MW00974520

TABLE OF CONTENTS

WRECKED
Chapter One
Sydney

I eased into the chair, my coffee cup in my hand. I had overdone it at the gym the night before, trying to push my leg presses to the max. This morning, I was feeling the effects of my overzealous workout, to the point where I'd had to roll out of my bed this morning.

"Overdo it last night?"

I looked over at one of the officers, Luke, who had apparently just watched me lower myself in the chair.

"Shove it, Luke. You only wish you could press what I was."

Luke chuckled, holding up his hands.

"Whoa. Syd. Don't take it personally. I was just wondering if you needed a massage later on, that's all."

I threw a pencil at him, a grin on my face. Luke was one of the officers that I actually liked here at Cibolo Police Department, and, while others would view his comment as sexist, I didn't. Luke and I had already gone down that road, the handsome officer trying once or twice to get me to date him.

While Luke was gorgeous, I wasn't interested. I wasn't back in Cibolo to shack up with the first man I laid eyes on. I was here to focus on my police career and build a reputation here.

Better than my last reputation.

Heaving a sigh, I brought my cup to my lips, allowing the hot liquid to warm my insides. Most would say that I was crazy, coming back to my hometown, but the badge on my chest gave me the support I didn't really need for people to take me seriously. All my life, I had been quiet and unassuming, not one to be noticed in a crowd, and spent the majority of my younger days in my room, with a book in my hand. I didn't have many friends growing up, nor did I care to.

I had just wanted to survive.

And then… well, I had become notorious overnight.

"Warren! In my office!"

I shook out of my thoughts, nearly upending my coffee all over my uniform, as the chief's voice cut through the air. I set the cup on my desk, wincing as I stood and walked to his office at the back of the department. Chief Turner was a heavyset man with a storied thirty-year career in law enforcement. When I had applied for this job, he had not wanted to hire me, stating that people who worked in their hometown tended to turn a blind eye on the happenings. I had promised him that I had no intentions of doing that. I would uphold the law in every aspect, doing my best to make Cibolo safe for the next generation.

Most of all, I had no intentions of giving anyone a break here. They hadn't done it to me back then, and while I was not bitter about that any longer I knew that it was a dog-eat-dog world in the small Texan town.

Why would I treat them any different?

"You yelled chief?" I asked innocently, sitting on the worn leather chairs in the stifling office.

The air conditioning had been acting up again at the station, and no number of fans were going to blow out the warm, humid air. It was only eight in the morning, and I was already sweating under my bullet-proof vest.

"Funny, Warren," Chief Turner said, narrowing his gaze at me. "I have a case for you."

I sat up just bit straighter in my chair. A case? I had only been with the department for four months, not planning on getting anything but the beat trails for at least a year. While I longed to be a detective one day, I knew I would have to work my way up in this department to get that privilege.

Chief Turner drummed his fingers on the scarred wooden desk while I waited for him to say something, anything, knowing he was biding his time.

And making me go insane.

"I debated on giving this to you," he finally said, leaning forward.

I could smell the pipe tobacco he liked to smoke, the heat starting to become stifling in the small office. I was going to need another shower before this day was over with.

"But this could be your big break," he continued, pushing the file to me. "And I think you have it in you, Warren, to be me one day."

"T-thank you sir," I stammered, surprised.

"You're welcome," he said gruffly. "Don't let me down Warren. Remember that oath you took."

I nodded, my heart racing in my chest. This was my moment to shine for this station, to cement a new reputation in Cibolo. Eagerly I grabbed the file and opened it, only to find one sticky note.

The chief chuckled as I read the name on the sticky note.

Amy Travis.

Oh, I knew that name.

"You didn't think it was gonna be that easy, did you Warren?"

I swallowed, shutting the file.

"I wouldn't imagine it to be chief. What do you need me to do?"

If he was surprised, he didn't show it.

"Ms. Travis is here right now. I have her in one of the interrogation rooms. She's looking for her missing sister. I need for you to find her."

I nodded tightly, standing. He was testing me. Well, I was going to show him that I was smarter than he thought I was. I was going to solve this missing person case faster than any other man in this department and prove to him that I could be chief one day.

"Thank you, sir."

"Good luck," he said, dismissing me.

I walked out of the office and toward the interrogation rooms, clutching the folder in my hands. Amy Travis was the oldest child of Grant Travis, a well-known leader of one of the many bike gangs that were in and around Cibolo. The Devil's Horsemen MC was a prominent gang in our area, fierce but not as deep into illegal dealings as many of them were.

I hated them all.

Straightening my shoulders, I kept on toward the room. It didn't matter. Every citizen of Cibolo, no matter how corrupt, deserved our full attention, and I couldn't hold it against them. I had grown up in a far different manner, in a loving household that sheltered me as much as it could from the horrors of reality.

But now, I knew all too well what the world brought and how it could shatter someone in an instant.

"You can do this," I whispered to myself as I reached for the knob to the room.

I had overcome so much to get here, and I wasn't about to allow this stop me. Pushing open the door, I looked at Amy Travis. She was older now, her long hair draped over her shoulder and hiding the tattoo that covered one shoulder, the end barely sticking out under the curls. She was dressed in a tank top and ripped jeans; her feet clad in boots that were stretched out in front of her in a relaxed pose.

But it was her eyes that were wary, moving over me as I walked in the room and shut the door. There were layers of hardness to her, some I knew she had built around her to protect herself from her father's choice of profession.

"Ms. Travis, I'm..."

She cut me off with the wave of her manicured hand.

"I know who you are, Sydney. You look well."

So, that was how it was going to be.

"So do you Amy," I said, pulling out the chair across from the table and seating myself. "How is the family?"

"Dad is good," she said with a sigh. "But Hayley is the reason I called Chief Turner."

Hayley was Amy's younger sister, a hellion even when I was here six years ago. She thrived in the limelight of who her father was and didn't mind using that name to get her what she wanted.

"Hayley's missing," I said flatly, putting two and two together.

Amy nodded, losing some of her bravado. I could see the underlying worry in her eyes now, the lines of exhaustion on her face. Despite what Amy's family stood for, I sympathized with her. To have a family member missing had to be devastating and, knowing what the Travis family dealt with, had to be even more of a concern. One of the other gangs could be using her as leverage, which didn't bode well for Hayley's sake.

There were things I had seen of what could happen when a family member got caught up in this gang war, and it wasn't pretty.

I pulled out the pad that was tucked in my shirt pocket, finding my pen.

"Tell me what happened."

Amy blew out a breath.

"You know Hayley. She's always running her mouth, boasting about who she is and what her father can do. I've told her to shut her trap more than once, that someone was going to use it against us one day, but would she listen? No of course not. She likes the attention she gets, and now it could be her downfall. Stupid, stupid girl."

I listened to Amy, catching the undertones of sadness in her voice. She was truly worried about her sister.

"Has anyone contacted you or your father?"

She shook her head, looking down at her nails, which were painted fiery red to match her lipstick.

"No. The last person to see her was her friends when they were at the mall two days ago. They said she got in her car and drove off. S-she never made it home."

I jotted down the specifics, though my stomach twisted at that thought of what the young girl could be going through.

If she was even still alive.

"Who do you think took her?" I asked softly as Amy sniffed away the tears in her eyes.

Amy laughed hollowly.

"You tell me, Sydney. Anyone could want to make a name for themselves by snatching Grant Travis's daughter. The cartel, the brotherhood, the brigade; they all have it out for our family, wanting to be on top of this area."

I shifted in my seat, knowing that unfortunately she was right. We had a number of lethal gangs in the area, some that made my skin crawl to think about. There seemed to always be a turf war going on, over who could make the most waves in the communities without getting caught, and I wasn't about to remind Amy that her father was one of them. While they weren't into some of the heavier stuff, such as sex trafficking, they were still no angels.

But that still didn't allow me to be their executioner. I had a missing girl who should be home with her family, and I would do everything in my power to find her.

Dead or alive.

"I'm sorry," Amy said quietly after a moment. "I'm not giving you much to go on."

"It's okay," I offered with a small smile. "I've had worse to go on, honestly. I will do my best to find Hayley, I promise."

"Thank you," she said, her expression softening. "Listen, I know we haven't ever been friends, but I do appreciate you looking into this. Chief Turner said you were one of the best here, and I… well, I want to find my sister."

"I know," I answered, feeling some of the pride well up in my chest. "I will do everything I can Amy."

She nodded and slid a card across the table.

"Here's my cell. Please don't put it anywhere on your paperwork. I'd like to keep that part as private as possible, along with this case. If word gets out that Hayley is truly missing, it could mean bad times for us, Sydney. I can't allow that to happen."

I tucked it into my pocket for later, knowing what she meant.

"You won't have to worry about it."

"Good," she said, standing.

I watched as she looked at her expression in the two-way mirror, wiping away the rest of the vulnerability she had just shown.

"Oh, one more thing."

I stood.

"What's that?"

She turned, a grin on her red lips.

"I know what happened to you all those years ago, and I promise I don't care. I just want to find my sister."

A shock vibrated through me, but I refused to show any weakness.

"Well, I'm glad that you are still interested in old news."

Amy placed her hand on her hip, regarding me with an interested look.

"You hide it well, Sydney. Don't let them get to you again. It's not worth it."

"I'll call you with any updates," I said instead, opening the door.

I didn't want to talk about my former misgivings. That was none of her business, and I had moved past it.

After all, I had come back to Cibolo to face my demons. Not many people could say the same.

"Thanks," she said, moving past me.

I waited until she was down the hall before I released a pent-up breath, the room still filled with her expensive perfume. She thought what everyone else did about me. It was fine. I couldn't ignore the fact that it had happened, nor could I run from it.

Walking out of the room, I forced myself to turn toward the task at hand. Finding Hayley Travis. Amy had a right to be scared about her sister's wellbeing. My gut reaction was that she had been taken by a rival gang; which one, I didn't know.

If that was the case, they would use and abuse her to prove a point, driving her father mad with the knowledge that his baby girl was being tortured for her secrets in some of the worst ways imaginable.

It had to be a parent's worst nightmare, no matter how bad the parent was.

Tapping the folder on my hand, I walked back to my desk. I would start putting out feelers to my contacts, see if anyone had heard anyone bragging about kidnapping Hayley. At some point, they would show their face, a slip up that would implicate them in the kidnapping, and I hoped I would be there to arrest them and bring Hayley home.

One way or another.

Chapter Two
Zack

I sat in the comfort of the office, my knee shaking anxiously. I didn't like being in there, especially when I had no fucking idea why I was in there to begin with. The summons this morning had come out of the blue, a text message that had gotten me out of bed and dressing as quickly as I could. When one was summoned by Grant Travis, you didn't make him wait a minute longer than you had to.

But I had been waiting now for an hour, attempting not to show my irritation at the fact. One of Grant's right hands stood not too far away, making sure that I wasn't going to do anything other than sit there, which was also making me uncomfortable.

As if I would steal anything in this office, from the hand that had fed me all those years.

Wiping my palms on my jeans, I sat back in the chair, wondering how much longer this was going to take. I had been part of the Devil's Horsemen MC all of my adult life. At eighteen, I was a rogue kid, with a rap sheet to match. Petty theft, burglary, disturbing the peace, and even one indecent exposure, was all part of my colorful teenage years, and there weren't many who thought I would even make it out of them.

But a chance encounter with Grant Travis had changed all that.

And now I belonged to a family, a brotherhood that had each other's back, regardless of the situation. I served them loyally and without hesitation, working my way up in the ranks to be one of Grant's trusted go-to men when he needed something carried out.

The door opened, and I exhaled a breath as Grant stalked into the room, walking over to his collection of liquor that he was known for.

"Whiskey?" he asked, his back to me. "Or something stronger?"

"I'm good, thanks," I said as he poured himself a glass.

He chuckled as he turned to face me.

"Too much alcohol last night, eh? I heard you took two of our lovely ladies' home with you."

I grinned.

"They were twins. Twins always stick together."

Grant let out a laugh, shaking his head as he rose his glass toward me.

"Touché, Zack, touché. I forget what it means to be young and full of cum."

I gave him a nod, looking at the president of the DHMC who had somehow held the position for twenty years. He had survived numerous attempts on his life and had always come out on top, and in today's world that was a feat that could not be rivaled. With the other gangs closing in on Cibolo, we were fighting on a daily basis.

One of the most recent skirmishes had been just the day before, when me and a few other members had gone south in search of a rogue biker who had decided to sell his secrets to the highest bidder. Little had we known that the members of the Caballeros de Los Muertos gang were manning one of their secret hideouts for their greatest trades: humans.

It had taken a great deal of explanation on my part to get us out of there with no bullet holes, though my neck had still tingled with concern as I had ridden away.

Hence the twins last night, 'given' to me by one of the other men who had been present as his show of gratitude.

I hadn't turned them down.

Grant let out a heavy sigh as he collapsed in his chair, his drink still in his hand.

"You know, there are days when I wish that I had stuck with what my parents had wanted me to do."

"What was that?" I asked, curious.

"A doctor," he laughed, shaking his head. "My father was a doctor, my mother a nurse. It was only fitting that I go into the medical field. Funny how life takes a turn, isn't it?"

I nodded. Had Grant not taken me under his wing and made me a part of this brotherhood, there was no telling where the hell I would have ended up at.

More than likely prison.

"I'm sure you are wondering why I brought you in here today," Grant finally said. "I need a favor."

"You got it," I said instantly.

Grant looked at me, a wry grin on his face.

"Just like that?"

"Just like that," I answered evenly.

I owed him my life and a great deal more.

"I've always liked you, Zack," Grant said slowly. "So, I'm hand-picking you for this favor. If you fail me, I can't guarantee what I might do. Do you understand?"

I nodded. I knew that we all lived by the seat of our pants around here, and if I failed Grant, I would want him to kill me.

Good thing I never failed.

Grant stared at me a moment longer before looking away, staring at the wall.

"Hayley has gone missing."

I loosened a breath. Hayley Travis was well-known to the clubhouse. She had her father under her thumb, and there wasn't anything that he didn't give her.

That, and she enjoyed the attention of the men at the clubhouse. While no one was brave enough to touch Grant's daughter, she loved to tease them to the brink of nearly doing so, only to see what her daddy would do. She had tried it on me once or twice, but I had scared her off each time. I had no interest in getting tangled with her.

That would be a sudden death.

Now, though, she was missing, and Grant was going to send me to find her.

"Shit."

"Yeah," Grant said, shoving a hand over his thinning hair. "She's been gone two days, and nobody has seen her. I'm afraid that… hell, I don't want to think about it. She's got to be somewhere, and I'm betting you can find her."

"I will," I said, clearing my throat. "Any idea who has her?"

"The Caballeros de Los Muertos is a good guess," Grant sighed, the thought etched on his face. "I… hell, I pissed them off last week, stopping one of their shipments when they crossed our path."

I was surprised, but not at all shocked. We typically didn't get involved with another's shipments, unless we wanted a full out war.

"So, you think this is retaliation?"

"Your guess is as good as mine," he shrugged, rubbing a hand over his face. "Her mother wants me to go to the cops, but I don't need the cops sniffing around here, not focusing on finding her and more on busting me."

I understood that. While we weren't one of the harshest clubs, we still dealt with some illegal shit that would land all of us in prison for quite a few years. The cops in the area, including the feds, had been itching to nail something concrete on us for years, but every time one of us was caught on something petty the legal counsel Grant employed got us off scot free.

It drove the local cops insane.

Grant looked over at me, and I saw the emotions flickering in his eyes.

"Go find my baby and bring her home, Zack. Alive or dead, I need to have her home."

Hell, I hoped it wasn't the latter. Without another word, I walked out of the office, my stomach churning at the thought. While Hayley was a pest, she was still a somewhat innocent young woman caught up in a mess all because of who her father was. I knew Hayley was tough, but being in the hands of the Muertos would make anyone crazy.

Rolling my shoulders, I walked through the clubhouse and out to my bike, knowing where I was going to start my search. There was one person who knew Hayley's whereabouts better than anyone else, including her father.

The ride over gave me time to think about my next moves and what I would do to bring Hayley home. I had given up a great deal of myself to be part of this brotherhood, to be seen as someone that they could trust, and I wasn't about to give that up as well.

Grant had been clear about his intentions if I didn't.

I pulled the bike up to the small house not far from the clubhouse, shutting off the engine and looking at the façade for a moment. She hated living here, and she had no qualms about telling anyone who listened. Her father lived behind the clubhouse, in a large house that couldn't quite be considered a mansion, though I had seen the interior.

More money had been put into that place than I would ever see in my lifetime.

But here, I believed, she was just refusing to accept that her father would make her stay here, in this house.

Not that she did for the most part. No, Amy Travis spent much of her time at the clubhouse, trying to prove to her father that she could hang with the rest of us. We all knew it, and I suspected that Grant did as well but refused to subject his oldest daughter to the harsh biker world.

Grant was likely going to lose that hold on her one day.

Climbing off the bike, I walked up to the door. The door opened before I could knock. Amy stood in the doorway, dressed in a tiny tank top and ripped jeans. She was a beautiful woman and, as much as she hated it, was off-limits just like her sister.

"Zack," she said with a smile. "Funny seeing you here."

"Amy," I acknowledged with a grin. "Can we talk?"

She eyed me before stepping out of the way, allowing me to walk into the house. I had been here many times before, dumping Hayley off when she'd had too much to drink and didn't want to take her home to her parents.

"Have a seat," she offered, pointing to the leather sofa in front of the TV. "You want a beer?"

"Thanks," I said, walking over to do as she had asked.

Amy walked into the kitchen and emerged a short second later with two beers, handing me one.

"What brings you over this way, Zack?" she asked, perching herself on the couch's arm. "Surely not for pleasure."

I grinned and took a swallow of the beer, letting the cool liquid slide down my throat. It was hot as balls outside today, the ride over nothing but a blast of hot air the entire way. The chill of the air conditioning started to cool me down and I looked over at her.

"I'm here because of Hayley."

Her grin faded, and she looked away, tapping one long fingernail against the bottle.

"Why?"

"Your father wants me to find her."

"Shit," she whispered, running a hand through her long hair. "Doesn't he know I'm handling it?"

I drained the bottle before setting it on the coffee table.

"What do you mean you are handling it?"

She looked over at me.

"I went to the cops this morning. They are assigning someone to look into it."

"Shit," I swore. This was the one thing that Grant hadn't wanted to happen. "What the hell, Amy?"

She stood up, tear in her eyes.

"I want to find her, Zack. I-I didn't know he was going to assign you, or I might have not done it, but she's out there somewhere, and I… what if she's dead?"

I heard the pain in her voice and lost some of my anger. She was scared. Hell, I would imagine Grant was as well.

"It's fine. I'm sorry. I can see why you did what you did."

"I didn't want to," she said in a little voice, looking nothing like the strong woman I knew she portrayed. "But I didn't have a choice, Zack. The officer… they are going to do it under wraps. They promised me."

I stood, cracking my knuckles. Just fucking great. A cop sniffing around the business. That's all I needed. Well, I would handle them. Most of the cops were on Grant's pay roll anyway, and all it would take would be a bit of scaring to have them look the other way while I dealt with this myself.

And if they sniffed too hard… well, I couldn't be responsible for what might happen.

"You'll call me if you get any word, right?" I asked Amy.

She nodded, gripping her beer.

"I will. Even if the officer calls me, I'll pass it along to you. I-I'm glad he gave this to you."

I nodded and walked toward the door.

"Stay out of the way, Amy. I got this."

She followed me to the door, her fingers drifting the back of my shoulder as I reached for the door.

"You sure you can't stay for a little while, Zack? I can help relieve some of that stress."

I laughed.

"Amy, you know that's not going to happen."

"Just thought I would ask," she muttered as I pushed open the door. "Stay safe, Zack."

I didn't answer, walking out to the bike and climbing on. It would be easy to take Amy up on her offer, knowing there would be no strings attached. She would likely be fucking amazing in bed, but… hell, I enjoyed my balls and was keen on keeping them. I might be Grant's current favorite, but I was in no mood to push my luck.

Gunning the engine, I pulled out of the driveway and headed south, toward Muertos territory. If they did have Hayley, I would have to go into the fray to find out information on her. I would have to put boots on the ground, by myself, to find out where they might be hiding her and what they wanted. They hadn't taken her without planning on using her against Grant.

I would need to find her before they started doing so.

I just hoped I didn't get myself killed in the process.

Chapter Three
Sydney

I checked my gun before sliding it into the holster strapped to my ankle, pushing my jeans down to cover it. I couldn't very well wear my side piece and badge where I was going, but I wasn't stupid enough to go in there empty-handed.

Actually, if the chief knew what I was doing right now, he would likely hang me by my boots. I was taking a huge risk going into this place without backup, but I couldn't afford for them to be tipped off.

So, I was going in as a girl looking for a good time. To play the part, I had forced myself into a tight-fitting shirt that showed off some of my best assets, the jeans molding to my ass likely to draw some sort of attention from the bikers. I had let my hair down and even applied just the barest touch of makeup, something I rarely did anymore.

After all, criminals could care less what I looked like, and the Texas heat was libel to melt the damn thing off before the end of the day.

I drove past the biker bar before parking the jeep down the road a way, not wanting to call attention to myself. I didn't own a bike, nor did I care to ride on one, so my jeep was the only option I had to keep the suspicion down.

That, and I had to keep my nerves at bay. I was nervous, more so than I thought I would be. Up until now I hadn't taken on a case by myself, nor had I decided to throw myself into this sort of danger just to break a case. I was a good cop, one that followed every direction to the tee, and had been known to be the rule-follower all through the academy. I didn't like shaking things up and kept it as real as I could.

But this… I felt like I was out of my wheelhouse. Sure, I had been around bikers in my teenage years, seemingly unable to not be around them, given our small town.

It didn't mean I had talked with them. Or pretended to flirt.

Squaring my shoulders, I started the hike up to the bar, noting several bikes out front. I was going to start with each gang until I heard something about Hayley and, given the history between the DHMC and Caballeros de Los Muertos, it was a good one to start with. The Caballeros de Los Muertos were known for their human trafficking, not only from Mexico, but also from the US into the Mexican country. While the border patrol struggled to control the trafficking, it still was a rampant business, one that made a lot of money.

I hated it. Of all the things that went on in my hometown, I hated the trafficking. Innocent lives destroyed as they were grabbed off the street and forced into the sex slave industry. Families ruined, innocence lost, and suffering that was unimaginable to the everyday human being. I had worked on more than one detail that had brought in a victim of sex trafficking, and to see the suffering in their eyes nearly tore me apart.

It was one of the reasons I had come home to Cibolo.

Drawing in a breath, I pulled on the handle of the door and walked into the dimly lit building, the smell of unwashed bodies and beer assaulting my senses. The building itself was crude and warm on the inside, with the laziest of fans attempting to circle the air above me. There was music pouring out of speakers mounted to the wall, tuning out the sound of the pool table in the back. The entire place was smoky, and I found myself blinking rapidly to dispel the tears that gathered in my eyes.

A tired-looking woman in a tube top and jeans eyed me as I walked up to the bar, seating myself on one of the worn stools there.

"Are you lost, honey?"

I shook my head, giving her my best sly smile.

"Lost? Depends on your definition of lost."

Her gaze narrowed, and she leaned forward, placing her hands flat on the scarred bar.

"If you are here looking to get into trouble, I suggest you leave. These men will eat you up and spit you out before you have a chance to blink. Take my advice, honey, get the hell out of here while you still can."

"Who's this, Brenda?"

Brenda swore under her breath as I turned to face a huge man with a shit-eating grin on his face, most of his teeth missing from his mouth. His nose was crooked, and there was a deep scar down the side of his face, disappearing into a scraggly beard that covered the lower half of his face. He wore the colors of the Muertos, and I sat up straighter, giving him a saucy smile in return.

"I'm Paula," I cooed, sticking out my hand. "Brenda was just getting me a beer."

"On the house," the man said as he fell onto the stool next to me. "I'm Pablo and I run this joint. Brenda's my old lady."

I kept the smile on my face. If I could have run into anyone during this covert operation, I couldn't have picked this one out any better. I tapped my fingers on the bar, inching them ever close to the arm that Pablo had rested there.

"Well, now, maybe you can show me a good time."

His grin turned feral, and his hand casually touched my thigh, brazenly squeezing it.

"Oh, we can do more than that."

Brenda slammed the beer on the bar, and we both jumped. The look on her face as she looked at Pablo was almost comical.

"Here. Drink it and get out."

"Shut the fuck up," Pablo sneered, raising a fist at her. "Get back to your job. I will take care of our guest here."

"I warned you," she muttered toward me before walking away.

I maintained my gaze on Pablo as he pushed the beer in front of me, his grin not fooling me in the least. Worst case scenario was that he liked to torture women like me, and in that case I would need that gun later on.

Best case scenario was that he was some sort of teddy bear, which I didn't see even coming into play. I was dealing with a dangerous man and needed to tread lightly if I wanted to keep my life.

"So," I said, fiddling with my beer, attempting to look nervous. "Doesn't seem there is a lot of women in here."

His hand stroked my thigh, and I had never been so happy to be wearing jeans in all my life.

"We don't and not as good looking as you. Maybe we can talk you into staying for a while?"

"I don't have anywhere else to be," I said softly, winking at him. "You know a friend of mine told me about this place. Said she had a really good time here the other night."

"Really," he answered, his gaze narrowing.

I swallowed, wondering if I had stepped over my bounds too quickly. I wanted to get my information and get out, but without raising suspicion.

And I might have just done that.

Chapter Four
Zack

I climbed off the bike and walked toward the door, knowing I was about to cause some shit in this place. For today's visit, I was not wearing my vest or any identifying markers to show my allegiance, but if someone recognized me… well, there would be hell to pay.

Still, if Muertos had truly taken Hayley, then I would need to infiltrate their ranks to find out.

And the only way to do so would be to go into the snake's den.

Taking a breath, I walked in, scanning the crowd inside instantly. I was on high alert, knowing to watch my back in enemy territory. There was a woman seated at the bar, her laughter drowned out by the loud music playing from the speakers. Next to her was Pablo, Carlos Juarez's right-hand man. Carlos was the leader of the Muertos, a man who had no mercy for anyone that messed with his operations. I knew I'd be damn fortunate to walk away that day.

Something about the woman drew me closer, and I felt the room shrink around me as I realized who she was.

What the fuck was she doing here?

Ignoring them for the moment, I stalked over to the bar and motioned at the bartender.

"What can I get you?" she asked briskly, her eyes sliding back to Pablo.

"A beer," I answered, leaning on the bar.

When she brought it, I tipped her with a hundred-dollar bill, her eyes widening before she pocketed it quickly. With a motion of her hand, she stomped over to Pablo.

"I'm going to smoke."

"Go, get the hell out of here," Pablo said, not even once looking over at me. "I'm busy."

I took my cue to walk down the hall that led to the bathroom, grabbing the bartender by the arm as she exited the bar.

She didn't even resist as we walked into the men's room, me leaning up against the door to keep from anyone barging in. She lowered herself to the floor and I stared at her.

"What the fuck are you doing?"

"Making it look official in case someone walks in," she muttered, reaching for my zipper. "What the fuck do you want to know?"

I swallowed as her hands brushed my cock inside of my jeans. I wasn't interested in what she had to offer, far more interested in what the fuck Sydney Warren was here for. She was a jolt from the past, one that I hadn't anticipated on seeing ever again after what I did to her.

But she was here, in the last place I thought I would see her, and now I had to make sure she didn't die either.

Shit this had gotten complicated.

"Have you seen another girl around here lately?" I finally forced out, staring down at the bartender.

"Besides the bitch at the bar you mean?" she asked with a sigh. "No, I haven't. Women aren't stupid enough to hang around here. I think that's a cop out there, and if she is, she's playing with fire."

Sydney? A cop? Oh shit, now that would be icing on the cake.

"I'll take care of her. Are you sure you've not seen any woman around here that doesn't belong? What about with Pablo?"

She sighed and stood, brushing off her jeans.

"I swear it. No one different than the other whores he keeps company with. Are you done yet? I gotta get back."

I stared at her, finding no reason for her to lie about what she told me. Hayley wasn't here, nor had she been here. It was a dead end.

"Here," I said, pushing another hundred toward her. "Get the hell out of here."

She laughed harshly as she tucked the bill in her bra.

"And do what? You're stuck just like I am."

I moved aside and let her go, walking out behind her. She was right. She probably knew more than most, and if she did leave, they would kill her to protect their secrets.

But now I had another issue to deal with. Walking back to the main room, I sat down at the bar again, looking at the back of Sydney's head. Sydney Warren. I couldn't believe it. Of all the women in my life that had come and gone, Sydney was about the only one who had latched on and stayed with me.

Even if I had ruined her life.

I also hated that. It was a defining moment in cementing my brotherhood with the DHMC, one that I couldn't take back.

Shit. Why was she here? Whatever it was, it couldn't be good. Still, my eyes traveled down the back of her, taking in how her curves were hugged by her outfit, her long hair draped over her shoulder and exposing the nape of her neck. There was much I remembered about Sydney from that one night, much more than she probably realized. I remembered the feel of her skin under my fingers, the way she had gasped as I'd shown her more than she had ever seen before.

Hell, that was almost eight years ago, and I could still feel it.

Shaking out of my thoughts, I noticed one of the bikers from the pool table eyeing me. I cursed under my breath as I realized it was one from the other afternoon. He laid down his pool stick, and I stood, cracking my knuckles. There was about to be a fight, and not only did I have to get my ass out of there, I had to get Sydney's as well.

This was not what I had imagined would happen.

"Devil trash," he sneered, pulling out a knife. "I thought I told you to stay away from us."

I held up my hands, giving him a slight grin.

"I don't listen very well."

"No, you don't," he said, tossing the knife between his hands. "And now I am going to gut you from head to toe."

Chapter Five
Sydney

I was in trouble.

Pablo's hands inched higher on my leg, and I gritted my teeth as he boldly swept them across my center, a leer on his ugly face. I would have to get out of there and fast, or I would end up in a situation I might not be able to get out of.

"Devil Trash."

Pablo's hands halted, and he was up on his feet in an instant, causing me to swivel around to see what the ruckus was. My breath stilled in my chest as I realized who was the center of attention. It couldn't be.

One of the bikers was holding a knife toward him, murder in his eyes.

"I thought I told you to stay away from us."

Zack Hale held up his hands and grinned, cockiness exuding from his expression. I knew that cockiness, and it had been my downfall, the reason I had left Cibolo.

Why, oh why, did it have to be him?

"Fucking Horsemen," Pablo swore under his breath, reaching for his knife.

I knew I had just a short time to react, pulling my gun from my holster and pointing it at the ugly biker.

"Now, now. I think this isn't a fair fight."

He eyed me, disgust crossing his face.

"You're a fucking cop."

I nodded, keeping the gun level as I slid off the bar stool.

"I am and you, my friend, are going to stay right there or I put a bullet through your chest."

His expression was murderous, but to my great relief Pablo didn't move.

"And now I am going to gut you from head to toe."

I winced as I heard the scuffle start to ensue behind me, my heart in my throat. I couldn't believe that Zack was there, my curiosity more than piqued, but I couldn't help him either. The moment I turned my back or showed any sign of weakness to Pablo, I would be dead.

A hand touched my arm and I nearly dropped the gun.

"Come on cop," Zack whispered in my ear. "Time to go."

My gun still trained on Pablo, I allowed Zack to guide me to the door, not breathing lest I accidently pull the trigger and kill someone. My heart was beating wildly in my chest, more so from Zack's light touch on my elbow than the danger I was in. A familiar shot of electricity shot down my spine. It had been… what, eight years since that night? Surely my body still didn't remember it.

Oh, but my heart sure did.

We stepped out into the blinding sunshine, and I turned quickly, tucking my gun in my waistband.

"Come on," I urged grabbing his arm. "My jeep is this way."

Surprisingly, he didn't object, and I tore off toward the jeep, glad for the running I had picked up. There were shouts behind us, but I didn't stop, jumping in and revving the engine as Zack climbed in. I heard the bikes fire up behind us as I threw the jeep into gear, pulling out with a squeal onto the highway. My foot pressed down on the gas, and we shot down the road, putting a few miles ahead of the bikes before I turned off into a copse of trees, cutting off the engine.

My heart in my throat, I waited until the bikes flew past before letting out a breath, resting my head on the steering wheel. I had done it. I had outrun the bikers.

"Fancy meeting you here."

I looked up, pushing my hair out of my eyes. Zack was seated in the passenger seat, a grin on his gorgeous face and I wanted to slap it off him. He had ruined my plans. He had been the reason I was holding bikers at gunpoint and running for my life.

"You nearly got me killed."

"Oh no, darling," he drawled, kicking his leg up on the dashboard. "You were about to do that yourself. What the hell were you doing there anyway? Are you fucking crazy?"

I frowned. He had no right to ask me those questions. That, and he had nearly gotten a public officer killed today.

"Give me your hands."

He arched a brow.

"What are you doing, Syd?"

"That's officer Warren to you," I bit out, reaching into the center console for a pair of zip ties. "And I am arresting you."

"Arresting me?" he laughed, wiping a hand over his face. "For what, Syd? For saving your ass? That should look really good on your report."

"Give me your hands," I repeated, not wanting to deal with this right now.

Oh my God, this was Zack Hale in front of me. He was the one person I hoped to never see again, though I knew deep down I would eventually. Cibolo was too small of a town.

"I'm not playing, Mr. Hale."

"Mr. Hale, huh," he said with a chuckle. "So, it's going to be like that?"

I gestured to his hands, and he held them out, allowing me to slide the zip ties over his wrists and cinch them tight. Once I had done so, it felt foolish. Clearly Zack could break out of them if he really wanted to. But instead he sat back, and I gunned the engine, pointing the jeep back toward town.

Only then did I release a breath, the excitement starting to wear on me. I had gotten nothing out of Pablo, accomplished nothing but picking up the one man I didn't want to see.

It sucked.

And why did he have to look so darn hot? I kept my eyes on the road, picturing in my mind his gorgeous features, the way his biceps strained against his dark t-shirt. And that grin… God, that grin had weakened my knees more than once.

I hated it. I didn't need that sort of complication in the investigation. I didn't need to see him and have all those feelings rush up to me that I had hidden deep in my soul.

Zack Hale had broken my heart once before, but he wasn't going to get anywhere near me or it this time. I was smarter, older, over the fact that he had smeared my reputation and dragged me through the mud for his precious biker gang.

I wasn't bitter at all.

Chapter Six
Zack

Well my day had gone to hell.

Shifting in the seat, I fought the urge to strain against the zip ties, not wanting to scare Sydney by popping them. She was taking this very seriously, and while I knew she didn't have anything to truly hold me on, I was here because I wanted to get to know this woman.

Selfish, I know.

"So," I started as the jeep rumbled down the road. "When did you get into town?"

"None of your business," she shot back, her hands gripping the steering wheel. "Just, how about sit over there and be quiet, will you?"

I grinned. Sydney the meek, mild girl I knew back then was gone. In her place was a woman who had my curiosity piqued. "Come on Syd, we know each other. Don't be like that."

She made a sound as she turned to the right.

"W-we don't know each other, Zack. If you did... well, never mind. You have the right to remain silent, you know."

Oh, I knew.

"You look good, Syd. When did you become a police officer?"

Again, silence. I leaned back on the seat and turned to look at her, taking in her profile and trying to imagine her in a police uniform. Sydney as a cop. I would have never guessed she would go down that road, fit more for a quiet, unassuming position like an assistant.

But she was a gun-toting, badge-wielding donut eater. Great. We were on either side of the law. Wait until the guys heard about this. No doubt they would give me hell for it, expecting the situation I found myself in to be the first of many now that she was back in town.

I deserved it and more from her.

The town-limits came into view, and I sat up.

"You know you don't have anything on me, Syd."

"'Officer Warren'," she forced out as she turned the jeep into the parking lot. "And even if I don't, I will relish in booking you in."

I leaned over, catching a whiff of her coconut shampoo, a familiar smell that had my cock stirring. Seems some things had stayed the same with her.

"I think you like the idea of having me in that tiny room."

She threw the jeep into park, and I nearly hit my head on the windshield.

"We're here," she said sweetly, hopping out.

I growled, more so because she had just turned me on than pissed me off.

Had she always had those balls, and I had been too blind to notice?

Climbing out, I didn't resist as Sydney led me up the stairs and inside, straight to the interrogation room.

"Whoa, Warren! Is that your new attire? Smoking hot!"

"Shove it," she growled as we walked past the officer.

He turned to check out her ass, and I growled this time, giving him my best damn hard-ass stare. That was my ass, not anyone else's.

The thought hit me like a ton of bricks. Claiming Sydney? Hell, she wasn't even talking to me, much less interested in where we'd left off. I had ruined her damn life with my antics and likely broken her heart in the process.

"In here," she said, holding open a door.

I walked in, waiting for her to shut the door before taking a seat at the table. It wasn't the first time I had been in a room like this, and I imagined it wouldn't be the last. Sydney sat across from me and it gave me time to look at her, taking in her gorgeous features. God, those eyes could slay a man from across the room, though I didn't see any innocence in them any longer.

I had taken away that innocence.

"What?"

I grinned.

"Damn, it's good to see you, Sydney."

She flushed, crossing her arms over her chest.

"You do know that you are under arrest. You have the right to remain silent. Anything you say or do can be held against you in a court of law. You have the right to an attorney."

I interrupted her.

"Stop. I know my damn rights. Can you at least cut these damn things off me? They are starting to cut off my circulation."

She heaved a sigh and got up, walking around to my back. I heard the snap of the tie and felt the blood rush back to my hands, bringing them forward to rub my raw wrists.

"Thanks."

"What were you doing in that bar?" she asked immediately, as she came back around the table. "I want answers."

I looked at her, her full cop mood doing a number below the belt. Shit. Would she be like that in bed now?

"You first. I belong there much more than you do."

"That's none of your business," she said, not sitting. "And I ask the questions, not you."

"Alright," I said, relaxing in the chair. This was fun having her interrogate me. "Fire away."

"Why were you at the bar today?"

"Business."

"What kind of business?"

"Club business."

She growled.

"I need more than that, Mr. Hale."

I leaned forward, bringing my hands together on the table.

"I can't tell you any more than that, Officer Warren. And it's 'Zack'. I think we are far from those formalities."

"This is an interrogation," she said through clenched teeth. "Not a friendly chat."

Unable to help it, I pressed on, wondering how far I could push Sydney. I was getting under her skin.

"Come on Syd. It's been a while. How did you get into this police shit?"

She sighed, loudly.

"Listen, Zack, I need to know why you were at that bar today. It's very important."

It was then I realized that Sydney was the cop Amy had been referring to. Shit. I didn't need her in the middle of a potential turf war between us and the Muertos. I could find Hayley without her help and probably quicker than she could as well.

"Syd, listen. You don't know what you are dealing with. Get off the case, tell them you can't do it."

She eyed me.

"What are you talking about? What case?"

I swallowed. I couldn't give myself away. There would be more questions than answers if I did.

"Whatever you were hunting in that bar. Don't go there by yourself again. If I hadn't been there..."

"I would have been just fine," she retorted, clearly angry that I thought she needed help. "I've been just fine without you all this time, and I will continue to be, Zack. I don't need you."

"There was a time when you did."

Her eyes widened before her mouth flattened in a thin line.

"Don't go there."

Oh boy, I had really pissed her off now.

"So, you haven't forgotten."

For a moment she looked as if she could hit me. But the more I pushed her, the farther she got from her questions, her prying, and that was what I was looking for. I needed for her to forget the reason she had brought me in to begin with.

"You're right," she said after a moment. "I haven't forgotten what you did. I will never forget what you did."

Ouch! I hated the tone of her voice, the hurt that shimmered in her eyes before she blinked it away. I had been a bastard back then.

"Syd..."

A knock on the door silenced me, and Sydney stomped across the room to open it, revealing Chief Turner.

"You, my office. Now," he directed toward Sydney.

"Hey chief," I said in an easygoing manner. "Long time, no see."

"Shut up, Hale," Turner growled as Sydney followed him out the door.

Once she was gone, I let out a breath, my shoulders slumping. The day was shit. I hadn't gotten any information on Hayley and got myself arrested by Sydney in the process.

That, and she was refusing to talk to me about anything other than police business. I knew she hated me. She had every right to hate me. Hell, I hated myself once the rumors had started to spread and Sydney had left town after her graduation, a place I should have been, cheering her on.

I had screwed up royally, stepping on the people that mattered the most to get where I was at today.

I was happy, wasn't I?

The door opened, and Sydney entered again, looking defeated.

"You're free to go."

I stared at her.

"What?"

"You heard her."

My head swiveled as Don Monroe, our legal counsel for DHMC walked in, a huge grin on his face. Short and fat, he was every inch the sleezy lawyer you would see on TV. But he was damn good at finding loopholes in the system, keeping us out of prison and in the good graces of the police department.

"Don, how did you find out?"

He nodded to Sydney.

"All you have to do is step inside this station and I'm aware. She doesn't have anything to hold you on, Zack, so you are free to go."

I eyed the officer that was fuming in the corner.

"No hard feelings?"

"Just go," she said with a wave of her hand.

I stood and walked to the door, trying to think of something to say to her. There was so much between us, so much I probably should say to clear the air, but the words just didn't feel right.

That, and with an audience it wasn't the appropriate place or time to do so. There would be a time, however, that we would talk about what happened eight years ago.

"Good to see you, Syd. I'm sure I will be seeing you around."

She didn't answer as I walked out, following Don out of the station and to his fancy Cadillac.

"Can I take you somewhere. Zack?" he asked, looking around. "I don't see your bike."

I pulled out my cell.

"I'll call for a ride, thanks."

Luckily, the bike I had driven to the bar was a loaner from the club, a piece of shit that could be used and left if need be. I doubted it was still in one piece after today.

"Well, alright then," he answered, climbing into his car and driving off.

I stared after him, debating on whether or not I should go back into the station and corner Sydney. She was playing with fire, and I didn't want to come across her dead in a ditch somewhere in the near future, all because she was sticking her nose into where it didn't belong.

"Shit," I muttered, firing off a text message before shoving my phone in my pocket.

What a freakin' hot mess. She wasn't going to listen to me any more than the man on the moon at the moment. I was far from being on her good side. In fact, no member of the DHMC was on the police's good side.

And now I had a cop I had a history with on my tail, working on the same case I was.

I needed to talk to Grant, to see what he wanted me to do about this. It wasn't going to be as easy as I had first thought, knowing that at every turn Sydney would be there, attempting to arrest my ass again.

I would never get anything done.

The sleek car pulled up and I opened the door, sliding into the cool exterior, a welcome relief from the Texas sun. I had to get Sydney to somehow see that I wasn't the bad guy in this.

Chapter Seven
Sydney

How could my life take a total one-eighty in the span of a few hours?

I sat at my desk, staring at the notes I had compiled, my thoughts scattered. I had interviewed some of Hayley's friends, not getting much from them that I hadn't already gotten from Amy. I had also checked on her cell phone records, but those were closed to me unless I could get her father's approval.

It must be nice to hold that kind of power.

Still, the events of the day were in the back of my mind constantly. Why had Zack been there at that bar? What were his ties to this case? He had let it slip about a case, and I suspected that he was working on something with Hayley's disappearance.

But couldn't prove it yet.

"Warren! Get the hell out of here!"

Sighing, I gathered my notes and tucked them into the folder. It was later than I normally liked to stay, but I couldn't shut off my brain.

Partly because of the case, partly because of my run-in with Zack.

"I'm leaving chief."

He didn't answer as I walked out of the station to my jeep, throwing my things into the passenger seat. Now that the doors were back on, I could smell Zack's cologne, my stomach flipping over at the thought of him sitting in that seat. God, it had been so long since I had seen him, though every once and awhile he would drift through my thoughts, more so after I had come back home.

Cutting on the engine, I pulled out of the parking spot and headed toward home, biting my lip as I did so. After the fiasco with Zack,

I had stuck it out until I graduated, making the first big decision of my life to move out of state. My parents hadn't stopped me but had sold their house and done the same in support of my actions.

I would never be able to repay them for what they had done for me during that time. They could have turned their backs on me, believed the rumors, and stayed here, but they hadn't.

In Oklahoma, I had attended college my first two years, getting my criminal justice degree before applying to the police academy. There, I had strived to be an overachiever in all areas, attempting to prove to myself and others that I wasn't the girl they had made me out to be. When I had told my parents I was taking a job in Cibolo, they had seriously considered admitting me to a psych ward. I would be stupid to go back there.

But here I was, and though the wounds had never fully healed, I was going to make a difference in this town.

Rolling my shoulders, I turned left toward the little house I was renting. I didn't know if it was going to be permanent or not, and the house had been in my price range. Besides, it had a fabulous tub that was calling my name.

With a sigh, I pulled into the driveway and climbed out, grabbing my things. A bottle of wine might go with that bubble bath. I was tired, my mind tired from the day's events and what I was going to do about Zack.

God, Zack Hale! I still couldn't believe the run-in I had experienced with him. He was still beautiful as sin, filling out his muscular body far better than he had the last time I had seen him, with tattoos running up both arms. Back then, he had been the bad boy, a few years older than me and way out of my league. I had been nothing but a nerdy, awkward girl with no friends and fewer love interests.

In fact, I hadn't as much kissed a boy until I met him.

Sighing, I pushed open the door to the house and deposited my stuff on the couch, walking to the kitchen for that cold bottle of wine I knew was in there. The day that Zack had approached me was forever etched in my mind, a memory that wasn't quite as bad as the rest of them.

***

I walked out of the library, clutching my books to my chest. Two months left until graduation. I was so ready to be done with school, to be done with the immaturity that high school brought. The guys were only out for one thing, the girls pretty much obsessed with the guys and their own reflections.

There were times I thought I was the only one worried about grades and passing my finals.

Thunder boomed overhead, and I hurried to my car, searching in my purse for my keys. I had stayed longer than I had planned, and I knew my parents would be looking for me to be at home for supper.

Finally, I succeeded in getting the driver-side door opened and dropped the books in the passenger seat before sliding in, putting the key in the starter.

Nothing.

"You have got to be kidding me," I muttered, attempting to turn it again.

Nothing happened, and I tried not to panic. I didn't have a cell phone, not really needing one, and the librarian was locking up as I walked out.

Great, just great.

A tap on the window caused me to jump, and I turned to see someone standing at the driver's side.

Not someone. The hottest guy I had ever laid eyes on in person.

"Hey, you need some help?"

I bit my lip, debating on whether or not to roll down the window. He looked... well, huge from my vantage point, with an easy grin on his face. My heart fluttered in my chest as I took in his gorgeous good looks.

He clearly wasn't a high school student.

"Come on," he coaxed. "You need help, I have jumper cables. I'm not going to kidnap you."

Seeing no other choice, I rolled down the window.

"I can't get it to start."

"Probably a dead battery," he said, pointing to a truck parked not too far from me. "I'm just going to pull up in front of you and we will get you jumped off."

I nodded and opened the door, watching as he ran over to the truck as the rain started to fall. This was not working out like I wanted it to at all. I snatched my umbrella and rolled up the window, stepping out of the car as he pulled in front of my car. Suddenly, I felt bad watching him climb out in the rain, popping the hood of both of our vehicles. He was helping me and getting soaking wet in the process.

The least I could do was help.

Walking over to him, I held the umbrella over both of us. He looked up and I forgot to breathe as our eyes met. Oh, this was not good at all.

"Thanks," he said after a moment, hooking the cables to his truck. "I appreciate it."

"I'm Sydney," I blurted out as the rain fell around us.

He looked at me and grinned, my heart pounding in my ears as I took in the sight.

"Zack."

***

A loud bang shook me out of the memory, and I looked around, half expecting to see something on fire.

When I didn't, I walked to the living room, frowning as I noticed the small hole in the front window. Shit! It was a bullet hole.

I pulled my gun from the holster and got low to the ground, fully expecting a barrage of bullets to follow. When they didn't, I reached for my cell, dialing the chief instead of dispatch.

"I just had someone shoot at my house," I rushed out as soon as he answered.

"What?" he asked, the sound of dishes clinking together in the background. "Did you say a shooting?"

"Just one shot," I breathed, pushing myself against the wall in the seated position.

"Do you want lights and sirens?" he asked, breathing heavily into the phone.

"No," I said, thinking of who could want me dead.

I doubted it was the case, just a scare tactic. But still… if I had been sitting on the couch.

"I bet it's the DHMC," Chief Turner replied. "You arrested one of them today. They don't take too kindly to being arrested."

I thought about Zack and our conversation today. He hadn't acted pissed. He had… well, he had enjoyed it for the most part.

"I-I don't think it was them."

"Warren," he said in a low voice. "I know who you arrested today, and I know your history with him. Don't let that cloud your judgement."

I frowned, hating the fact that the chief even had to say anything about that. I was over Zack. I wasn't protecting him. Hell, I had arrested him today!

"I'm not chief."

"Good," he said. "So, what are you going to do about it? You wanna fill out a report?"

"No," I replied, standing. I knew exactly what I was going to do. "I'll handle this one off-the-record."

"Don't get yourself killed," he said before ending the call.

I drew in a breath, staring at the small hole in the opposite wall, where the bullet had come to rest.

They thought they had scared me.

All they really had done was piss me off.

* * *

Thirty minutes later, I pulled up in front of the DHMC clubhouse, staring at the bikes that lined the yard. It was already night. The sound of laughter and music drifted out of the building that was well known to the rest of the community. One didn't just walk up to the clubhouse without an invite, but I was going to create one. I needed to know if Zack or anyone else had just attempted to kill me and tell them to back off in the process.

If I needed to speak to Grant Travis, I would. I needed his cooperation to stay the hell out of my way while I tried to find his daughter and not make it more complicated for me to do so.

Drawing in a breath, I checked the gun in the holster one more time before climbing out. I had come prepared tonight, my gun snugly under my arm, another tucked in my boots. At the last moment, I had forgone the bullet-proof vest, not anticipating any gunfire tonight. I wanted them to see that I was serious, but not a threat.

Not yet. If they were the ones that shot at my house tonight… well, then the game changed.

As I walked up to the clubhouse, I kept my eyes straight ahead, reminding myself over and over that I was here for one specific purpose. I was here for Hayley Travis.

Luckily the first person I ran into was Amy.

"Sydney?" she asked, stopping in her tracks. "What are you doing here?"

"I'm here to see your father," I said evenly, looking directly at her. "It's important."

Amy staggered back.

"I-is it Hayley? Did you find her?"

I shook my head.

"I haven't yet, but… well, I need to talk to him about his interference."

She looked at me for another minute before realization dawned in her eyes.

"You're talking about Zack," she said flatly. "He's the reason you're here."

"Yes and no," I answered, hating the fact that I had to even admit that. "Is he working on Hayley's case as well?"

"Why don't you just ask me?"

I turned to find Zack behind me, his massive arms crossed over his chest. My heart thudded in my chest as it always did whenever he was around, and I swallowed against the flood of emotion that was threatening to overrun me. I was here to do a job.

"Are you working on Hayley's disappearance?"

He didn't answer, grabbing my arm instead and walking me into the clubhouse. I barely had time to register the jaw-drops as I passed, the whispers and laughter that followed causing my cheeks to burn. If he was intentionally trying to embarrass me, he was succeeding.

I was going to kill him.

Zack walked me into a small room and shut the door, leaning against it.

"Why did you do that?" I countered, crossing my own arms over my chest.

His eyes followed the subtle motion, and I fought against not undoing my arms, knowing his eyes were on my breasts.

"I'm a police officer, for God's sake."

"And it's going to get your ass killed," he said evenly, no hint of emotion on his face.

Well that wasn't true. His jaw was clenched so tightly that I was surprised he wasn't breaking teeth.

"Why are you armed to the teeth, Syd?"

I straightened my shoulders, comforted by the fact that I could shoot him if I wanted. No one would blame me, thinking I had gone rogue after years of embarrassment. Hell, Don might even represent me.

"You have a gleam in your eye. I don't like it."

Shaking out of my devious thoughts, I shifted my stance.

"Again, I'm allowed to carry my weapons and rarely go without them. Did Grant order a hit on me tonight?"

Surprise registered on Zack's face.

"What? What the hell are you talking about?"

"Someone shot at my house tonight," I said, my voice not shaking, even though I was inside. "They missed."

"Fucking hell," he swore. "Of course not. I wouldn't... no one from this clubhouse would dare attempt to kill you, Syd. Shit. What kind of person do you think I am?"

I wasn't so sure. There had been a time I thought he was the best person on earth, and then he had shattered my heart and my reputation in one fail swoop.

The emotion must have shown on my face for he held up his hand.

"Don't answer that. I promise you. I would never. Grant would never put out a hit on you just for arresting me. I'm not that vengeful."

I watched him for a moment. He looked rattled at my news, at my accusation. Could I believe him? I wanted to. Despite the history between us, I wanted to not believe he was the monster that had been portrayed to me. I wanted to believe that, still locked inside, there was some resemblance of the guy who had made me feel like the most special woman on this earth.

Most of all, I wanted to know he cared, even if it was just a tiny bit.

"I believe you," I forced out. "But you need to be honest with me. Are you working on Hayley Travis's disappearance?"

He eyed me for a moment before blowing out a breath.

"Hand-picked by Grant to find her. You must be the cop Amy gave the case to."

Chapter Eight
Zack

Sydney was here, in the clubhouse.

Sydney had almost died tonight.

God, what a rollercoaster of emotions she had just put me through.

I ran a hand through my hair as I stared at her, not sure what to do about her. A part of me wanted to push her against the wall and search for bullet holes myself, my rage barely contained at the thought of someone shooting at her.

The other part of me wanted to lock her up in this damn room and throw away the key. At least she would be safe.

"I am," she finally said, dropping her arms to her side.

I noted she had changed out of her outfit from earlier, wearing jeans and a shirt that molded to her breasts. Hell, with that holster and her dead-ass stare, she was turning me on something fierce.

"That's why I was at the bar today. I was trying to follow a lead."

"Me too," I admitted. I might as well air it all now that she had figured it out. "I have to find her, Syd. I can't back off."

She blew out a breath, her hands on her hips. Her shapely hips that would fit damn good in my hands. Shit, she was bound to notice the tent in front of my pants if I didn't focus on something else and quick.

"I can't either," she finally said, looking put out about the thought. "This is my job Zack. I can't just let it go."

She called me 'Zack'. That had to be a start to something.

"I'm not asking you to. Maybe we should pool our resources and work together."

Her eyes found mine and I was surprised to see the hesitation in them.

"Do you think we can?" she asked in a small voice.

"We can try," I offered.

If we did work together, I could protect her from whoever had taken a personal vendetta against her.

I could find a way to apologize.

She thought about it for a moment before shrugging her shoulders.

"Fine. We can team up, but I am going to need you to tell Grant to back off. If he wants his daughter found, I need to focus."

"It wasn't us," I reminded her again, put out that she thought it could be.

If I found out that it was one of the DHMC, they would be dead even if she wasn't hurt.

"You can trust me Syd."

The moment the words were out of my mouth I wanted to shove them back in. Her eyes widened, and I knew exactly what she was thinking about, how the last time I had said those words had led to ruin for her. What she didn't know was that I had meant them then as well. Circumstances had led to the ruination.

She lifted her chin, and I found myself begging for her to respond.

"Please don't say that to me again," she said softly with a steel undertone.

"Got it," I forced out, not wanting to fight with her right now.

There would be a time and place for everything, and tonight was not that time.

"I need for you to leave now, so I can talk to Grant."

"I want to talk to him as well," she said stubbornly.

"Not tonight," I growled, opening the door. "Give me this time, Syd."

She looked at me for a moment.

"Fine, but don't hide anything from me, Zack. If I find out you are, this truce is over with."

"Noted," I said, motioning toward the door.

Sydney walked out, and I followed her, shooting a dark look to anyone that dared to approach us as I got her outside and to her jeep. She climbed in and I shut the door.

"I'll be in touch."

"I-I'm living in Mrs. Green's old house," she offered, reaching into her console. "Here's my cell."

I took the card and tucked it into my back pocket.

"Thanks. I'm sure you can find my number in my records."

She shot me a dark look.

"That's not funny Zack."

I gave her a half shrug.

"It's true. Go home. Call me if you have any more trouble."

She started the engine and I stepped back, watching as her taillights disappeared in the distance. I wanted desperately to follow her, to make sure she got home safely, but I knew she would hate me for it. Sydney Warren had made it clear she didn't need me to protect her.

I just couldn't help but wonder who was going to protect me from her.

***

The next morning, I located Grant in his office, having his morning coffee. Amy was also there, and by the looks of their red faces their conversation had been quite heated.

"Got a second?"

Grant looked up, motioning me in.

"Sure. You have word?"

I shook my head, glancing over at Amy.

"I don't, but I do have some help from an unlikely source."

Grant's eyes narrowed.

"Sydney Warren. I heard she showed up last night, spouting some nonsense about us trying to kill her."

I didn't react, knowing that there were spies in the clubhouse that listened to every word that was exchanged there.

"I set her straight on that fact. She's agreed to work with me."

Grant looked at his daughter.

"Do you trust her?"

Amy shrugged, giving me a peculiar look.

"I guess so. I believe she will be looking out for Hayley's best interest. Chief Turner spoke highly of her, and I'm sure Zack wouldn't be wanting to work with her if he didn't trust her as well."

Grant sniffed, sliding his glance back to me.

"I know your history with her."

Hell, him and all of Cibolo knew of our history.

"So? That's exactly what you said. 'History'."

The leader chuckled, shaking his head.

"If I know anything about women, they never forget when they are wronged. Are you sure you want to do this?"

"I can keep the police presence to a minimum," I added, not caring what he thought about if I could handle it. "She will listen to me."

"Are we talking about the same person?" Amy asked under her breath.

I knew what she meant. The shy Sydney I had known was long gone and in her place was this woman I didn't know how to control.

"Fine," Grant finally said, waving his hand. "I want updates though. My daughter is out there, and I want to know who fucking took her."

"On it," I said before walking out.

With each minute we wasted, Hayley was in more danger. I needed to push to find her, and now that I had the resources from the police department, I might get it done in half the time.

The only problem was that Sydney was that resource.

I hopped on my bike and drove back to my house, located not far from the clubhouse. While I had been offered a room in the main house years ago, I was not like Amy. I wanted my freedom, my privacy, when I needed it. The place was small and ugly, but it was private.

Opening the door, I threw the keys on the counter and reached for the fridge, pulling out a water. That had gone better than I had expected and now that Grant knew I was working with the police, it gave me free-rein to be around Sydney. She had been a complication I hadn't expected, but one that I was glad had happened.

Unscrewing the top, I took a long drink, thinking about what might have happened if I hadn't made that mistake all those years ago. Sydney and I had something good going for a while there. She was so much more than just a gorgeous woman. She had made me want to be a better person for her.

That stupid fucking initiation.

I set the water on the counter, thinking about that night and how two words had changed my life and hers forever. If I hadn't uttered her name, I would have never gotten into the DHMC. She would have graduated from high school, and I would have been right there to congratulate her.

Then, as we had talked about, she would have attended the community college and I would have gotten a real job, one that could have supported us as our relationship grew. It would have been far from the white picket fence dream, but I could have made her happy.

We *would* have been happy.

I ran a hand over my face, feeling the weight of what I had done heavy on my shoulders. I had given up the one thing that had made me even remotely happy for this business, for this chance to be part of a brotherhood. At the time, it had seemed like the only thing that mattered.

***

I swallowed hard as I was sat in the chair, my vision blinded by the bandana on my face. I knew where I was, anticipating this day was coming, and now that it was here I couldn't believe my luck.

I was going to be a Devil's Horseman.

The bandana was removed but not the zip ties. As the room came into focus, the first person I saw was Grant Travis, the President of the club, flanked by numerous members.

"Zack Hale," he announced, a grin on his face. "Rumor has it that you want to be part of this club."

"It's not a rumor," I said, clearing my throat.

I could be one of these men. I could be the best man he ever chose.

"Well then," he said, sitting on the chair in front of me. "We have a series of tests you are going to have to pass to get in."

The rest of the room snickered, but I looked him directly in the eye, not caring what they thought.

"Bring it on."

"Big words," Grant mused, pulling out a knife.

I didn't flinch, not knowing what he was going to do with it. It couldn't be any worse than what I had already been dealt with in my life.

"First question," Grant said, testing the tip of the knife with his thumb. "Have you ever seen the devil?"

Oh many, many times. Every time my old man beat me as a kid, I saw the devil in him.

"He's never far away."

Grant looked at me, seeing something in my expression that pleased him.

"Have you ever spilled blood before, son?"

I shifted in the chair, keeping my gaze on the leader.

"More times than I care to mention."

I was forever getting into skirmishes on the streets. No one ever died, but they came damn close.

"I believe you," he said with a shrug. "There's something in your eyes, son, something that reminds me of me."

The others murmured amongst themselves, and I sat up straighter. Grant Travis had just given me the biggest compliment of my life.

"Last question before we get to the fun," he said, getting a rile out of the group. "Ever spill virgin's blood?"

Sydney's face flitted through my mind and I swallowed hard. I hadn't anticipated this question. What she had given me... it was not something that I wanted to share.

But if it meant getting me into this elite group, would I be willing to share?

"Yeah," I finally said, feeling a bit queasy from the question. "I have."

"Who?"

Shit. I was hoping that would be enough.

"Does it matter?"

Grant nodded, a gleam in his eye.

"It does. We need to make sure you aren't lying. Surely you can remember her name. Could it be Sydney Warren? Rumor is that you have been seen with her."

I wanted to hang my head. I would be giving away her own personal secret.

I didn't have to. Grant laughed as he stood.

"So, it was her. Get him up. Let's begin."

***

I shook out of the memory, feeling my stomach roll. I hadn't said her name, but it had been written all over my face. The initiation had consisted of cutting me over and over to see my tolerance for pain, getting me drunk, and letting the club women have their way with me. I didn't even remember that night for the most part, but when I woke the next morning I had the customary DHMC tattoo on my chest and a feeling of accomplishment that had lasted all of five minutes.

The rumors started nearly immediately, and the good girl I had known had been drug through the mud, labeled as a Horseman slut before the sun could come up. She had refused to even see me, and her dad had threatened to shoot me, Horseman or not.

I had walked away, not even attending the graduation or having the opportunity to apologize to her.

And it still was a rift between us. Though we had only dated two months, I had started to think of Sydney as my future, that I could meld both worlds together and be the happiest man in all of Cibolo.

I had been dead wrong on all accounts. Seeing her now, it made me remember what I had and what I had lost because I had been too blind to think it mattered.

My cell vibrated in my pocket and I pulled it out, my mood sour as I hit the button.

"Yeah."

"Zack," came Sydney's breathless voice. "Are you available right now?"

I was available whenever she needed me. Ignoring the rapid beat of my heart, I started toward the door.

"What's wrong?"

"Nothing," she said. "I-I captured a Muertos for speeding. I haven't brought him to the station yet, but I was wondering if you could help me interrogate him before I do."

She was brilliant.

"Where are you?"

She rattled off the address, the excitement in her voice making me think this could work between us.

In more ways than one.

"Hurry up," she said before ending the call. "I can't be gone much longer."

I shoved the phone back in my pocket and walked out of the door, choosing the truck over the bike this time. If I needed to take this fucker into the back woods, I would need something that could hold more than one person.

As I started the engine, a grin slid across my face. It had been some time since I had beat the truth out of someone, and I was in a mood to do so.

I just hoped Syd agreed and let me at him.

Chapter Nine
Sydney

I was nervous.

I watched the driveway to the warehouse, hearing the Muertos curse loudly and bang the metal chair against the floor, as if he could get the zip ties to loosen. I had tied him up tightly, holding the gun to his temple and threatening him within an inch of his life if he moved.

Everything that was against protocol, against what I should be doing.

But when he had flown past me in the jeep, I had pulled him over with the intention of telling him to slow down. Ten miles over the speed limit could warrant a ticket or an arrest, depending on the cop, and I had been feeling generous given that he checked out.

But when the flag had popped up about his involvement with the cartel, a thrill had run through me like a bolt of lightning. This was my chance. This was the big break we needed to find Hayley.

Finally, after what seemed like hours, a truck barreled down the driveway, and I knew it was Zack. My heart leapt into my throat as I recognized that truck, the same one that had been such a major part of our relationship.

He had kept the truck. I couldn't believe it. In the two months we had 'dated', I had ridden in that cab more times than I cared to count, done things toward the latter part, when it all fell apart, that would surprise everyone who had known me before the rumor spread.

And in that bed… well, I had lost everything, though at the time I had thought it was the beginning of something wonderful.

Zack pulled the truck to a stop and hopped out, jogging over to meet me.

"Are you alright?" he asked immediately, giving me a once over.

"I'm fine," I answered, snapping back to the present. "He didn't give me any trouble, honestly. Surprising what you will do if someone has a gun to your temple."

Zack grinned and my knees buckled slightly.

"Good girl. What do you want your plan to be?"

I looked at him.

"I-I thought I would take your lead."

He shook his head, that damn grin still on his lips.

"You're the cop. I'm the civilian you are pulling into your evil deeds. It's your call, Syd."

I was surprised. Not at his joke. Zack was horrible at jokes. He was deferring to my lead, letting me make the calls. He was taking me seriously as a cop, and I didn't know whether to laugh or cry about it.

"Alright," I said instead, thinking for minute.

He was going to be hard to crack. The cartel knew what happened to those who spilled the beans on their operations, and no jail cell would protect him from what they were going to do to him. The cartel had so many people on their payroll it made Grant Travis's look like a grocery list.

You couldn't trust anyone with a cartel member. I had heard of too many being killed under lock and key, when they should have been protected the most.

"Do you think he will recognize you?"

"I doubt it," Zack said slowly. "Why?"

I pulled the gun out of my holster, handing it to him.

"Don't fire it or I will have to answer a lot of questions. You are the bad cop."

"You are letting me be a cop?" he asked, surprised. "Do I look like a cop?"

I looked him over, letting my eyes linger on his body just a little too long. God, he was sexy. How far did those tattoos go? So many years had come and gone. It would be like learning a whole new body for me.

What was I thinking? I wasn't going to see Zack naked or be touching him otherwise.

"An undercover one," I forced out, not failing to notice the slight grin that he was giving me.

He knew what I was doing, and I should be ashamed.

I wasn't, in case you were wondering.

"I'll give it my best shot then," he said, checking the weapon. "Don't worry, Syd. I have no intentions of ruining your career. I know how hard you have worked for this."

"I… thanks," I said, stripping off my holster and undoing the top three buttons of my shirt. If I was to be the good cop, I wanted to look the part.

Zack watched every movement, my skin flushing under his intense stare as I let down my hair, fluffing it so that it fell over my shoulder. Normally when I was working, I kept it in a bun, too prideful to cut it yet.

The way that Zack was watching me, I was glad I hadn't.

"You ready?"

He swallowed.

"Damn Syd. You're gorgeous."

I rolled my eyes, though secretly I was thrilled he thought so. Maybe I still had some hold over him. There was a time I thought I had tamed the bad boy, showing him that good girls could be good for him as well.

Gah, I had to stop thinking like that! There was nothing between Zack and me anymore. I didn't care about him. I didn't love him.

"Come on," I said harshly, turning my back on him.

I didn't want these feelings.

He had broken my heart and I didn't think I could survive him doing it again.

The cartel member hadn't made much progress with his ties. The chair was several feet away from where I had put him, but nothing that would make me concerned. The warehouse was often used to store police raid gear, and the room I had put him in literally had nothing in it.

"You will die for this, cop!" he yelled, straining against his ties. "I will gut you myself."

"Now, now," I said in a soothing voice. "There's no need for that. Didn't I tell you I would let you go if you played nice with me?"

"Give me a knife," he growled, his eyes wild with rage. "I will play with you and make you scream."

His words had no impact on me. He was young, and what I knew about the cartel was that they marked their members with a brand, just above the collarbone. He didn't have the brand, which made me think he was a runner, nothing more.

Still, he would be easier to garner information out of. Runners were typically overlooked in a room when others were talking business, which made him far more valuable than pulling a top-ranking member. I pulled up a chair and took a seat in front of him, close enough for him to see that I meant business, but not close enough for him to head butt me.

"I need some information."

He spat on the floor, cursing me in Spanish.

"I will give you no information."

"The lady asked you for information," Zack said from somewhere behind me.

Even though I had given him a gun, I still felt safe having him here. In my heart of hearts, I wanted to believe Zack would never hurt me physically.

Emotionally, that was a different story.

"The Devil's Horseman," the cartel member cooed, a gruesome smile on his face.

So much for trying to pass Zack off as a cop.

"Working with the pigs."

"Damn right," Zack came over, holding the gun level to the cartel's face. "And I have no qualms about blowing off your greasy head."

"Now, let's just think about this," I said quickly, seeing the flash of panic in my prisoner's eyes.

Good. He was scared. It was my turn.

"I'm sure I can talk him down if you give me what I want."

"I won't give you shit," he said, his eyes on Zack and not me. "I hope you rot in hell, Devil."

Zack jammed the barrel of the gun so hard against the man's forehead that I winced. That was going to leave a mark.

"Tell her what she wants to know, or your brains will be splattered all over that wall behind you."

"I-I'm not afraid to die," he stammered.

I noticed he was sweating and grinned inwardly. We had him right where we wanted him.

"Give me something," I pleaded, leaning forward so he got a healthy look at my breasts. "Whatever you want to tell me. I know you are a smart man and don't want to die today."

His eyes flickered down the front of my shirt, and Zack swore under his breath.

"Anything?"

"Anything," I said, twirling a chunk of my hair with my finger. "I will be forever grateful."

"He's wasting our time," Zack cut in, pressing the gun into his forehead. "Let me off him so we can go."

I fought against rolling my eyes. No one said 'off'.

"Don't."

I looked up, seeing the man looking up at Zack with pleading eyes.

"I-I know about a hot package."

I scooted closer.

"What kind of package."

His eyes flickered between us, apparently trying to figure out which one he wanted to please the most.

"I don't know. A hot package is all I heard. Something important."

"Where?" Zack asked softly, not lowering the gun yet. "Do you have a location?"

The man swallowed hard, his Adam's apple bobbing up and down.

"I do. Uvalde. Today."

I sat back. Uvalde was an hour's drive from here.

"What time?"

He shrugged, careful not to move his head from the gun lest Zack got an itch.

"This afternoon. Nothing moves until the afternoon. Too hot for anyone to care."

He had that right. Zack lowered the gun and I stood, looking down at him.

"Thank you. He hasn't killed anyone in the last twelve hours. It's a record."

Zack didn't even flinch, though I saw a glint of humor in his eyes.

"Let's go."

I knew what he was thinking. The package could be Hayley. I looked at my captive.

"Don't go anywhere."

"You said you were going to let me go!" he whined as we walked away. "We had a deal!"

I kept walking. He would be alright until I got back. Then I would book him for the rest of the station to interrogate him. A cartel member, no matter their ranking, was vital to us stopping their trade. The chief would love to have him for a few hours.

Zack handed over my gun, and I picked up my holster just outside the door.

"We can take the truck."

I swallowed, looking over at the vehicle.

"I would rather take my jeep."

"What do you have against my truck?" he asked, his gaze narrowing. "It rides better."

That was the last thing I needed to hear.

"I'm the cop. We take the jeep."

He eyed me, finally blowing out a breath.

"Yeah, fine. Whatever."

I walked to my jeep and climbed in, firing the engine as Zack climbed in. This was our big break. If the hot package was Hayley, then we could potentially close this case today. The thought made me crazy with need to get there in a hurry. I wanted this over with and soon. The longer it drew out, the more I was going to have to be around Zack.

It wasn't good for my psyche.

Pulling out onto the main highway, I let the hot breeze blow through my hair.

"You did good back there."

He chuckled.

"It was fun being on the right side of the gun this time. You were great Syd. I-I didn't know how you would handle that situation."

I laughed. He had fully expected me to buckle under the strain.

"They don't teach you that in the police academy, that's for sure."

"I imagine not," he remarked, stretching out his legs. "I would have never thought you had that in you."

There was a time I would have thought the same thing.

"I've changed."

"I've noticed."

A warm flush spread through me as I heard his undertone, the sexy way he said those words. He wasn't just talking about my demeanor.

"What do you think the package is?" I asked, changing the subject.

"I'm hoping it's Hayley," he said with a sigh. "We need something solid for Grant."

I nodded, agreeing. I needed something to jumpstart this case in the right direction. I was tired of hitting those brick walls, and until that morning I hadn't been sure I was ever going to catch a break. After the attempt on my life the previous night, I hadn't slept well.

That, and dreaming of Zack and how it used to be. It was like my memories had decided to overwhelm me all at once, reminding me of what I had felt, what I had dreamed about when all was well and good between us. I had been that naïve girl, drawing hearts around our names, and pairing my name with his in my diary. I had dreams of the white picket fence and the two point five kids in the yard, with Zack by my side the entire time.

I had thought I could change him.

But it had all been just dreams. I hadn't changed the bad boy in him. I hadn't tamed him with my good-girl qualities and the way that I had fallen in love with him. I hadn't made him feel special, made him want to be with me.

All I had done was give him the ammunition he had needed to get into that damn clubhouse.

It irked me to know he had used me in that manner.

"What's the plan?"

Zack's voice broke through my thoughts, and I gripped the steering wheel, forcing myself back to the present.

"I really don't know. We can't go in guns blazing."

Zack chuckled.

"You know I have my own gun, right?"

I looked over at him.

"Why didn't you use yours then?"

He winked at me.

"I enjoyed holding yours far better."

I rolled my eyes.

"Are you serious? I bet you don't even have a permit for yours."

"Does that mean you will arrest me again, Syd?"

"Shut up," I growled, focusing on the road. We didn't have time to be flirting with each other. "What do you think the plan should be?"

He blew out a breath.

"I think we should scope it out. If it is Hayley, then we will have to improvise. I don't want you to get caught in a crossfire."

I noted he didn't speak about himself. The sudden thought of Zack covered in blood made me sick to my stomach. I didn't want to be leading him to his death either. Though I had thought about torturing him more than once during our time apart, I didn't truly want to do him harm. I would be stupid to think I didn't care about him. Zack had taken everything from me; my first kiss, my first sexual experience, my first love. There was always going to be a part of me that held some affection for him.

Oh, how I hated it!

"We will just see what we find then," I finally said, pressing my foot to the gas, urging the jeep on.

Neither of us were getting hurt today.

Chapter Ten
Zack

I tried to ignore the smell of Sydney's perfume as we lay next to each other in the dirt, watching the action below. Despite what I should be feeling, I was enjoying every moment with her. She was completely different to me, like a completely new woman, but there were moments that I saw the old Sydney in her. Like right then, as she nibbled on her bottom lip as she looked through the binoculars. There were many times during the time we had been together that she had done that, especially when she was nervous.

Hell, I was nervous. How she did this on a regular basis was beyond me.

"I see two men," she said softly, her voice barely audible over the wind. "I don't recognize them."

"Let me see," I said, reaching for the binoculars.

She handed them over without a word, and I slid them over my eyes, frowning as I recognized one of the men. Shit. It was El Pajaro. That was not good. El Pajaro was one of the chief human traffickers, at the top of the DHMC's hit list if we ever got a shot at him. I imagined he would be number one for the police department as well. The man was legendary in Cibolo and beyond, and rumor was that he had killed over one hundred men in his lifetime, though it was unknown how many of his human bargains had died as a result of being picked up by his men.

If he was taken down, the trafficking business would take a major blow.

"It's El Pajaro," I whispered, handing back the binoculars.

"*The* El Pajaro?" she hissed back. "Are you sure?"

I nodded, feeling the adrenaline start to build in my bones. Fighting El Pajaro was not going to be easy, as he was always accompanied by five armed guards.

"Crap," she said with a sigh. "If he has Hayley..."

Sydney's words died in her throat, and I swallowed hard, understanding what she couldn't say. Hayley could be long gone, traded multiple times by now. Her name, her connections, would mean nothing to her captors after she had left Pajaro's hands.

That was, unless he was planning on using her as leverage against Grant. Grant was going to be pissed to know that his daughter might be with this psycho.

"What's the plan?" I asked softly, my eyes on the man standing near the SUV.

The windows were dark, keeping us from seeing the cargo inside, and it appeared they were waiting on something.

Or someone.

"I don't know," Sydney said with a frown. "I don't want to engage unless we are sure he has her. As much as I would like to haul him in, I don't have the manpower."

I didn't take offense. Knowing Sydney, she would want this one done by the book, in case El Pajaro attempted to use a loophole to get out.

But if he had Hayley, I wasn't going to show him any mercy . I would shoot him where he stood and walk away with a grin on my face. This wasn't about taking out the cartel mercenary, this was about getting back Travis's daughter.

The sound of another vehicle approaching the site drew my eye, and I watched as the truck came into the picture, two men jumping out of the cab and carefully approaching the SUV.

"Here we go," Sydney muttered, pulling her gun.

I did the same, the weight of the butt comforting in my palm. The Glock had gotten me out of more than one skirmish in my adult life, and I rarely travelled without it.

Well, except the other day in the bar. I was glad that I hadn't had it on my person, or Sydney would likely have confiscated it.

We watched as the figures approached each other, their conversation in Spanish as they spoke back and forth about something. Were they bargaining for Hayley? My finger hovered over the trigger as Pajaro motioned at the SUV, his men walking back to open the door to the back.

This was it.

But instead of a human being, the men removed a large box from the back, lugging it toward the men with some difficulty.

"I bet it's drugs," Sydney said softly. "The hot package was drugs, not a person."

Relief flooded my veins. They didn't have Hayley. This was not a trade.

"Likely heroin."

That was the cartel's drug of choice, because of the money it brought in.

"We were so close," Sydney responded, lowering her gun. "I thought this was it, I really did."

"Minor setback," I said, looking at her. "Let's go before we are spotted."

There was no reason to rile up this exchange today.

She nodded and stood, brushing off her clothing. I rose to do the same, but before I could a shout went up and the rock next to Sydney exploded.

"Get down!" I yelled at her, grabbing her hand as I fired back.

She dropped next to me and joined in on the gunfire, her gun firing in rapid succession to mine. I had to get us out of here. We wouldn't have enough ammo to take on what was waiting down there for us.

"Get ready to run," I shouted over the gunfire, firing at one of the Muertos that was hiding out beside the SUV.

He yelped and went down, which opened up a very short window.

"Run!"

Sydney didn't hesitate as I covered her, firing as we backed toward the jeep. I heard her gun the engine, and I turned, covering the distance left to the jeep, and jumped in.

"Go!"

She pressed the gas to the floor, and we shot off, the sound of the gunfire fading in the distance as we flew over the desert. I set my gun on my lap and blew out a breath, my heart pounding in my ears. That had been close. We had been damned lucky not to be killed.

"Zack?"

I turned toward her seeing her pale face.

"Syd?"

"I think I've been shot."

The floor fell out underneath me as I saw the blood spreading along her rib cage, her hand covering the wound.

"Shit. Pull over."

She did so, and I hopped out, hurrying to the driver side, a thousand thoughts running through my mind. I couldn't lose her now. There were so many damn things I needed to clear with her, so many things she needed to know. Tears were in her eyes as I reached her, sliding my hands under her legs to lift her up.

"I-I think it's a graze. Oh God, it burns."

"I got you," I said, swallowing my emotion. "I'm going to put you in the passenger seat, so I can drive. Alright?"

She nodded, and I did just that, pulling off my shirt to hand to her.

"Put this on the wound and hold pressure."

She took the shirt and did as I instructed, the sight of the amount of blood on her causing me to freak out internally. She was not going to die today.

Hopping in the driver side, I tore off down the road.

***

It didn't take us long to reach my place, and I pulled the jeep in behind my truck, cutting the engine before retrieving Sydney from the passenger side. She didn't protest as I lifted her into my arms. I could feel the stickiness of her blood on my chest as I walked to the door. I knew I should have taken her to the hospital, but there would have been too many questions that I was certain she didn't want to answer right now. If it was just a graze, I could patch her up.

Kicking open the back door and not caring as the door frame splintered, I strode to the bedroom, depositing her carefully on my bed.

"Is this your place?" she whispered as I smoothed the hair from her face.

"It is," I said, keeping my cool. "Though I would like to have you in my bed for a far different reason."

Her eyes narrowed, and I knew that she wasn't focusing on her wound right now but was thinking about how to kill me.

"I'll be back. Don't move."

I strode to the bathroom, grabbing the supplies I kept under the sink. Dammit, why did Syd have to get hurt? My hands were shaking at the thought of her dying in that bedroom, though I knew she wouldn't. What if it had been worse?

I looked up and saw the blood smeared across my chest, the sight making me ill. That was Syd's blood.

"Shit," I swore, grabbing a few towels before heading back to the bedroom.

Sydney hadn't moved from the spot.

"I'll ask you one time. Do you want to go to the hospital?"

She looked at me, her eyes glazed with pain.

"N-no."

I nodded.

"Let's get that shirt off you, then."

I removed my shirt from the spot she was holding, easing hers up over her bra and pulling it from her body, wincing as I looked at the angry red welt on her right side. While it had bled like the devil, there was no signs that the bullet had actually penetrated the skin.

"It's just a graze," I forced myself to say, my tongue thick in my mouth. "It will hurt like hell for a few days, but I don't think you need stitches."

"Thank God," she whispered, looking up at the ceiling. "I'm a wimp when it comes to stitches."

I grabbed the gauze and placed some alcohol on it.

"This is going to hurt like hell, Syd, and I'm sorry."

She didn't say anything as I pressed the gauze to the wound, hearing her hiss in return. To her credit, she stayed perfectly still.

"Where else have you had stitches?"

"Busted my head open on the course during training," she answered, rubbing a hand over her face. "A dozen stitches along my hairline. It hurt like hell, but I didn't cry."

Hell, she was tough. This was not the young girl I had been so infatuated with all those years ago. There had been an innocence to Sydney that had kept me coming back for more, and I had stolen that innocence, hoping that some part of her would cleanse me of my bad upbringing.

Clearing my throat, I removed the gauze and applied a fresh one, using the medical tape to tape it in place.

"Do you want some painkillers?"

She shook her head, wincing as she rose to a seated position.

"Not right now. Thanks."

I looked at the now doctored side, the way her porcelain skin stood out in sharp contrast to the blood that covered it. She looked like she had been in a war, and it was all my damn fault.

"Syd."

She looked at me.

"What?"

It was now the perfect time to tell her how damn sorry I was. About everything.

"I'm an asshole."

The side of her mouth lifted.

"I know."

I chuckled, running a hand over my hair.

"I mean it. What I did to you… it was all wrong and I can't apologize for what happened."

There were no words, no amount of groveling that would fix what I had done to her, to the one person who had believed in me and seen something that everyone else hadn't. She had been the best part of me, and I had pushed her away.

Her grin faded, and I saw the emotions churning in her eyes.

"I'm not that girl anymore, Zack," she said softly. "And I haven't been for a long, long time."

"I know, and it's my damn fault," I interrupted, taking her hands in mine.

A jolt of electricity shot through me, but I ignored it. I didn't know what this was about, whether it was driven purely by the fact that Syd could have died today or because it was all finally coming to a head, but I had to tell her.

"Dammit, Syd, I took you virginity."

She flushed.

"I gave it to you, Zack. There's a difference. I… well, I was in love with you."

Hell, I knew that. She had told me that night, making what we did all the more special. I had never thought someone could love me, but she had, freely and willingly, without any thought to the bastard that I truly was.

"But," she continued, pulling her hands from my grasp and reaching for her shirt, "the club meant more to you, and you got what you wanted, didn't you?"

"Syd…" I started, not sure what more to say.

She was right, and it sounded fucking horrible coming out of her mouth. I had wanted badly to be part of the DHMC and had told her numerous times about it.

I just hadn't expected it to go down like it had.

She shrugged on her shirt, and I frowned as I saw the blood that raced across it.

"Let me give you one of mine," I offered pushing away from the bed. "You look like you lost a bad fight."

"It's nothing," she stated as I crossed the room and pulled one of my t-shirts from the drawer.

I turned back to her, my cock twitching as I looked at her sitting in my bed. How many times had I wanted to see that? How many times had I dreamed about her under me as I buried my cock in her warmth?

"What?"

I shook my head and walked back to her, handing her the shirt.

"Put it on. I'll take you home."

She eased the shirt on and pulled her hair out of the collar, letting it fall around her shoulders.

"This brings back memories."

I grinned.

"You wore my clothes more than I wore them."

A soft smile came to her lips as she fingered the hem of the shirt.

"Your clothes were always so comfortable."

I remembered; oh, how I remembered. I would pick her up down the road, so her parents wouldn't see the trash she was hanging around with, and we would go riding. Many, many times I would coax her into swimming in the lake, desperate to get my hands on her body.

She would shyly agree, but not before I gave her my shirt.

As if that had been enough to hide her body from my eyes.

And her wearing that shirt now… it brought back those feelings, the ones I had desperately tried to fight right up until that fateful night with the DHMC.

I took a step toward her, and she scrambled off the bed, wincing as she grabbed her side.

"I'm going to go home and clean up. Meet you back at the clubhouse?"

I hesitated.

"You need to go home and rest. This can wait."

"No, it can't," she fired back, her eyes blazing. "I'm fine. I will be fine, Zack. I'll meet you in two hours."

I didn't reply, and she left the bedroom, the sound of her footsteps echoing through my house, before her jeep started up and I knew she was gone. Hell. She wasn't going to listen to me.

I sat down on the bed, picking the remnants of my doctoring off the floor. I had patched myself up more than I cared to admit but patching up Sydney had been an entirely different feeling. That, and she clearly didn't want me to coddle her.

Or protect her.

I crushed the paper in my hand. She wasn't going to get hurt again. Not on my watch.

Hell, I couldn't go through that again.

Two hours later, I pulled the jeep up to the clubhouse, wincing as I accidently stretched my side the wrong way. I felt better after a hot shower and some Tylenol to kill the burning sensation. As much I wanted to sleep the rest of the night away, we still hadn't gotten any closer to finding Hayley, and I was itching for a breakthrough.

But first I wanted to lay down the law to Grant Travis. He wasn't helping at all. If it hadn't been for Zack, I wouldn't have gotten as far as I had today, but we had wasted our time for nothing. I wanted to make sure that Grant wasn't withholding information. As much as I disliked him, I wanted to find his daughter.

No surprise, Zack met me halfway to the door, looking as if he had just gotten out of the shower himself.

"How are you feeling?" he asked softly, his eyes raking over me.

"I'm fine," I forced out.

I didn't need him worrying about me. The moment between us hours ago had me rattled, wondering what life would have been like if he hadn't ever brought my name up to the DHMC and I hadn't been forced to leave town. Zack didn't seem like a settling-down type, but there had been a time in our relationship that I thought he would have, with me.

But that tattoo I'd seen on his chest as he had given me his shirt had reminded me what had come first in his life, and I was a fool to think there had been more to him, more to what he had wanted out of our relationship. Being labeled a slut, a biker slut at that, had torn me apart, turned people away not only from me, but also from my family. A biker slut was known to exchange sex for information, who's loyalty was above all to the biker gang she belonged to.

Though I never had any visible marks or tattoos, the label was there, and I had endured snickers and ribald jokes from guys who had never paid attention to me before, thinking I was easy and willing to give it up to anyone.

The marks on my soul had been permanent, and it was because of the man standing before me, attempting to apologize at every turn. There weren't enough words he could say to make that pain go away.

"I want to see Grant," I said angrily, angry at myself for letting Zack seep back into my life. "And I won't leave until I do."

Zack looked at me, his eyes full of emotion, but surprisingly he didn't say no.

"Come on."

I followed him, ignoring the looks as we walked through the clubhouse to an office in the back. It was a very nice office, but it was the man seated behind the desk, barking into the phone, that had my attention. Grant Travis. The man who had ruined my life, had pulled Zack from me and made him into the man he was today.

That was what Zack had left me for.

Grant looked up, and his eyes narrowed as they feasted on me.

"What the hell is she doing here?"

I stepped forward before Zack could answer.

"I'm here to know what you are hiding."

His hard stare cut through me, and I heard Zack swear behind me.

"What?"

I placed my hands on his desk, leveling with him.

"I'm trying to find your daughter, and you are not helping me. I nearly died today. What would that have looked like, I wonder?"

Grant looked at Zack.

"What is she talking about?"

"We had a run-in with Muertos," Zack offered up, his tone dark. "And Pajaro."

"Shit," Grant said, leaning back in his chair. "Don't tell me that Hayley is with that bastard."

"I don't know," I interrupted. "But if you know something about her, who has her, I need to know that. I can't help you if you don't give me that information."

"We need more men," Zack threw in. "If you want us to go after Pajaro."

Grant looked at us before shaking his head.

"I can't give that order. That would be a death sentence, us going after him. That would start an all-out war with the cartel, and I can't allow that to happen."

I couldn't believe it. He wasn't even going to attempt to go after the man that might have his daughter?

"Is that what you care about?" I asked. "This precious club? What about your daughter? What about her life? Does that not mean anything?"

"Don't you tell me what I care about!" Grant shouted, rising from the chair. "I built this club, not you or anyone else!"

"At what cost?" I challenged, not scared of him. "Your family?"

It wasn't just him I was talking about. Zack had done the same thing. I had been his family, and he had thrown me away.

"Get the hell out of here," Grant growled. "Before I put a bullet in your head."

"Go ahead," I said, crossing my arms over my chest. "But you know I'm the best shot at finding your daughter. I have resources you can't even begin to tap into, and if I disappear, then Hayley is as good as dead."

"Get her the fuck out of here!" Grant shouted.

Zack grabbed my arm and I allowed him to drag me to the door, knowing I had gotten under Grant Travis's skin. I had made him feel something, which had been the sole purpose of tonight's visit.

Zack didn't say anything as he dragged me out of the club, bikers literally moving out of his path as we walked outside.

"Get in the damn jeep," he growled, pushing me toward the passenger side.

I turned to face him.

"I will not be bullied, Zack. I have things to do."

He leaned forward, and I could see the anger in his eyes.

"Do what I say, Sydney, or I will give you to Grant and let him deal with you."

I wasn't scared.

"Where are we going?"

"You will find out when we get there."

***

Thirty minutes later, Zack pulled my jeep into the clearing, shutting off the engine. I looked around, surprised and not believing he had done this to me. This was not where I wanted to be, at all.

"Take me home."

He let out a breath before turning to look at me, his arm draped over the steering wheel.

"What the hell were you trying to do back there, Syd? Get yourself killed?"

I opened the passenger side door, the jeep suddenly too small for the both of us. Night was all around me, the stars twinkling overhead with the soft grass under my boots. This clearing brought back too many memories for me, and I did not want to be here, to break down in front of Zack.

This was our special place.

"Talk to me, Syd."

I turned to see Zack standing a few feet away, his hands in his pockets. There was nothing that even remotely resembled the kid who used to bring me here. That Zack had been darker, edger, but still had a tenderness about him that used to make me have all the feels.

This one… I had no idea what to do with this one.

"Why did you bring me here?"

He blew out a breath, looking around.

"I… hell, I don't know. It was the only place I knew you couldn't run from me."

I was tired of playing games. Marching toward the jeep, I ignored him.

"I'm going home."

He grabbed my arm before I got to the jeep, trapping me against the hood with his body.

"You are going to talk to me, Syd. What were you thinking, taking Grant on like that? Are you trying to piss him off?"

"I'm trying to get him to feel!" I exploded, feeling the pent-up rage start to boil over. "That's the problem with you bikers! You have forgotten everything you cared about except your precious club. His daughter is missing, and he doesn't seem to even care!"

Zack's eyes dilated, and his expression grew angry.

"Is that what you think? That I don't care anymore?"

I swallowed hard.

"I-I don't know what to think anymore, Zack."

He expelled a breath.

"Hell, Sydney, I wish I didn't care. Do you not know? No, I guess not. I came for your graduation night. I watched you celebrate with your family and knew I would just screw it up if I stepped back into your life."

My mouth dropped open as I saw the rawness on his face. Zack had come for me?

"But why?"

"Because," he said, looking away. "I didn't want you to hate me. I didn't give away your name that night. Grant guessed it. Turns out he'd had someone following us the weeks leading up to the initiation, attempting to find things to use against me. They just put two and two together."

"But you still went through with it," I said, emotion in my voice. "After the rumors spread, you didn't once attempt to come to my aid, Zack. Do you know what I dealt with? Do you know how disappointed my family was?"

They had never even once guessed that Zack and I had been involved together. I hadn't known how to tell them that I had fallen in love with the wrong guy.

His expression was torturous.

"I know, hell, I know. That was what I was doing there that night. I wanted to apologize to you, to your family for what I had done. I-I was going to tell them that I loved you."

My heart stuttered in my chest.

"W-what?"

His lips curved in a smile.

"You heard me. Hell, Syd, I was in love with you too."

I stared at him, my heart bursting past the walls that I had built up against him. All these years… not once had I thought he had loved me. I thought I had been a distraction for him, knowing that at some point it wasn't going to be forever.

But how I had hoped.

He reached out and lightly pushed my hair out of my eyes, his finger trailing down my cheek.

"You were a complete surprise to me, Sydney. You were the complete and total opposite of what I thought I wanted, but that day, in this field, I knew that I couldn't let you go."

"But you did," I whispered, feeling the pain of that day.

I remembered the panic of calling his cell after I had heard the rumor, how he had ignored all my calls and texts. I had cried non-stop for two days, realizing I had been used and cast aside.

"I know," he admitted. "And it was the stupidest thing I have ever done in my life. I don't want to lose you again. Ever."

I made a sound, and Zack's mouth slammed into mine, opening up a flood of emotions as I wound my arms around his neck. This was what I wanted. This was what I had dreamed about more than once since we had found each other again.

Zack growled and forced his way past my lips, his tongue torturing mine until I whimpered against his mouth. It was all wrong, but oh-so right.

His hand traveled down my body, cupping my breast, and I froze, pushing on his chest until he took a step back. There was hunger in his eyes, and I felt it all the way to the pit of my stomach.

"This..."

"This is right," he ground out, pulling his shirt over his head. "This is right, Sydney. Nothing else matters."

I took in his naked torso, my eyes drifting over the tattoo on his left pec. It was his stamp from the DHMC, the proof that he had gotten what he wanted. His eyes followed mine and he chuckled, crooking a finger at me.

"Come here," he said. "Look closer, Syd."

I stepped forward, my legs wobbly as I approached him, peering at the tattoo in the jeep's headlights.

"It's my initials."

Sure enough, at the bottom of the crude tattoo, there were my initials, hidden inside the tails of the tattoo.

"I had them added," he said softly, his voice laced with emotion. "Afterward."

Tears sprang to my eyes as I looked at Zack. He was giving me all he had, the proof that he had never forgotten about us, about me. Our worlds might have changed, but he hadn't.

Neither had I. I was still that girl with stars in her eyes every time I looked at him, not believing how lucky I was to be riding in his truck, wearing his clothes, touching his body.

He had been everything to me.

Reaching out, I laid a hand over the tattoo, feeling the heat come off his skin in waves.

"We aren't those people any longer."

He captured my hand in his.

"I know, and I don't fucking care. I'm still the man who dreams about you, who knows your body better than you do. I'm still that man."

I silenced him with a kiss, not wanting to talk any longer. He was right. He was the only man who knew this body, the only man that had ever made me sigh in wonder and happiness.

I was glad I had waited.

Zack lowered us to the ground, pausing just long enough to slide my shirt over my head. I met his gaze as his hands covered my breasts.

"Beautiful."

I touched his strong shoulders, sliding my hands down his muscular chest to his abdomen before they collided with the waistband of his jeans.

"I don't want to wait."

I had waited long enough.

He chuckled, laying back in the grass.

"Have your way with me, officer."

I laughed as I tugged on his button, tapping his hips so he would lift them.

"Still no underwear, I see."

"Nope," he grinned, bringing his arms behind his head.

I took a minute to marvel at his body, my breath shallow in my own chest. His tattoos curled around his shoulders in dark, thick lines, but somehow matched the rest of him.

"You're beautiful."

"I'm all yours," he said gruffly.

My panties flooded at the thought. He was all mine. He always had been.

His cock slid from under his jeans, and I grabbed it boldly, feeling him jump in my hand.

He was giving me complete control.

"Easy now," he said softly. "It's been some time, Syd."

I ran a thumb over the bulging head, sliding it down the shaft. Zack had taught me so much about pleasing him, and those memories were flooding back. I knew he hadn't waited on me, but, seeing him laying beneath me, it didn't matter.

Nothing in our pasts mattered.

Chapter Twelve
Zack

She was fucking killing me.

I gazed at Sydney as she stroked my aching cock, watching her eyes. It had been a long, long time since I had seen her rising above me, and my body quivered with the thought of her doing it again, reminding me why I had loved her for so long.

And I still did.

It wasn't just a feeling. It wasn't just because of the history between us or her initials permanently tattooed on my skin.

It was because she was in my soul, where she had always been.

Sydney released me, and I watched with bated breath as she rose in the headlights, removing her bra and bearing her beautiful breasts to me. My mouth watered at the thought of them in my mouth, but I refused to move. This was Sydney's night, not mine. I had brought her here, to our clearing, to show her that I hadn't forgotten and that I wanted to restart everything that had been between us.

The hell with everyone else for the moment.

She shimmied out of her jeans, and I thought I would blow it right then and there as I took in her naked form.

"You're fucking gorgeous."

She walked toward me, and I felt her hands run over my chest before she lowered onto my cock, her wet warmth surrounding my aching member.

"Shit," I whispered, reaching for her hips to guide her the rest of the way down.

The grass was itching my bare ass, but I didn't give a fuck.

Sydney was seated on my cock.

She let out a sound, and I growled, urging her to move.

"Ride me."

She placed a hand on my abdomen and pushed herself upward, shuddering as I slammed into her. God she was so wet, and I wanted to give her everything.

"Zack," she cried as she moved against me.

"Yes," I said through gritted teeth, fighting my own orgasm. Only Sydney could put me to shame like this. "Come for me, Syd."

She shattered around me, clenching me tightly as I pumped into her, the flood dousing me in wet warmth. I was right on the tip of my own orgasm, her sounds driving me crazy. The sound of our bodies hitting together drove me faster, and I groaned as I let go, her cries mingling with mine.

She fell against me, and I rubbed her back, our bodies sticking together in the nighttime heat. This was fucking crazy.

I loved it.

"I believe the last time we had a blanket," I said after a few minutes, my fingers drifting down her back.

She giggled against my chest, and I let out a breath.

"You are going to have grass in your ass."

"That's not the only place," I said, feeling the hard ground under me. "It was well worth it."

She propped her chin up on my chest and looked at me, the flush of her orgasm still shining in her eyes.

"This thing..."

"…is not wrong," I finished for her, touching her nose. "It wasn't wrong then and it's not wrong now."

"I know," she blew out a breath. "But what are we going to do, Zack? I'm a cop. You are a biker outlaw. We can't possibly carry on a relationship and not get in each other's way."

"Don't think about it," I said, tangling my hand in her hair.

She was saying all the right things. There were complications with us being together this time around, but I refused to think about them right now. Syd was here with me, and I wanted to savor in the moment.

"Tell me something."

"What?" she asked, her fingers tapping on my chest.

"Anything," I said, wanting to keep this going. I knew the moment we left this clearing this would be gone, and I didn't want to leave. "Do you still like mayonnaise on your fries?"

She laughed.

"Of course, I do. Do you still like hot sauce on your burger?"

I grinned.

"You know it. Puts a kick on the meat.'"

She shook her head, her eyes dancing with laughter.

"I swear, you are going to rot out your gut, Zack, by doing that."

I gave her a shrug.

"That was what attracted you to me in the first place."

"You wish," Sydney said.

I grinned, thinking about our first date. She hadn't thought I would come, and I hadn't thought I would have as much fun as I had.

***

"Oh, come on! Are you serious?"

I glanced at her in the passenger seat, taking in her jeans and top. There was nothing sexy about it, but I was holy turned on, wondering what color underwear she was wearing.

"I'm serious as a heart attack. I've never been."

She eyed me.

"Then you must go tonight. I can teach you."

Bowling was not the plans I had in mind. Hell, I hadn't even thought about anything but how she was going to thank me for starting her car that day, this date her way of showing her appreciation.

A thousand thoughts had run through my mind, but none of them were good and wholesome as she looked right now.

"Seriously."

"What?" she smirked, crossing her arms over her chest. "Are you too scared that it might mess up your bad boy image?"

Leave it to the goody two-shoes to call me out.

"Fine. I'm not scared. Do your worst."

And she had. For hours she cajoled me into bowling, my throw improving to where I could at least knock down one or two pins. At first, I had felt like a damn fool, but Sydney had this way about making me feel comfortable, and I found myself looking forward to her celebrations as she spanked me in each game.

"See, wasn't that fun?" she said breathlessly as we turned in our shoes and I paid for the games. "I told you."

"Alright you did," I answered as we walked out of the alley. Reaching over, I grabbed her hand, wrapping mine around it. "It wasn't bad."

She squeezed my hand back, giving me a soft smile.

"I promise it will get more fun the more you do it."

"Only if you do it with me," I said, surprising myself. "I don't want this to be the only date between us, Sydney."

We approached the truck, and I trapped her against the door, my hand sliding down to her hip.

"Tell me you want more."

Her eyes widened.

"W-what do you mean?"

"This," I answered, sliding my hand up her side.

God, she had more curves under that shirt than I had thought.

Her breath hitched in her throat, and I leaned forward, brushing my lips across hers. She tasted like the cherry coke she had ordered at the counter.

"You're fucking gorgeous."

She slammed her hands into my chest and caught me off balance. I stumbled back a few feet.

"What the hell?"

"Listen," she said, her voice wavering. "I'm not that type of girl. I'm sorry if you thought I was."

"Easy," I said, holding up my hands. "I'm sorry. I didn't mean to scare you."

Then it hit me.

"That was your first kiss, wasn't it?"

Her cheeks burned, and I felt a surge of pride. She had never been kissed. I was dealing with a complete virgin.

"Hey," I said, walking back toward her until I could tip her chin upward. "Don't be embarrassed. I think it's pretty fucking awesome."

She had never been touched. I was going to be the first.

But I would have to go slower than normal. She wasn't the sort of girl I was used to, who took over before you could even do so. Sydney was a clean slate, and I was going to be written all over her before she even realized it.

"Are you sure?" she finally said, searching my eyes.

My chest tightened as I saw the uncertainty in their depths, some of my earlier thoughts fading away. I didn't want to hurt her. She shouldn't even be associated with me. I was trash, with no future, and she was… hell, she was perfect.

"I promise. Can I try again?"

She nodded, and I felt nerves kick in as I lowered my head. Her first kiss had to be perfect.

***

"Hey, where did you go?"

I blinked out of the memory, seeing Sydney staring back at me.

"I was thinking about our first date."

She flushed.

"You mean our first kiss."

I nodded, my arm tightening on her waist.

"I was scared shitless to know I could screw it up."

"No, you weren't. You were only hoping to get in my pants that night."

Maybe at one time, but if she only knew how much she had changed me that night…

"And look where we ended up."

Sydney slapped at my chest and pulled herself up, the white of her bandage catching my eye as she searched for her clothes.

"Did I hurt you?" I asked, feeling like an ass for taking advantage of her tonight.

She had to be hurting.

She looked at me, before following my eyes, her mouth curving into a smile.

"No, I'm fine."

I pushed off the ground, swatting at my back to remove the grass before pulling up my jeans. This night had turned out better than I had hoped, though I wanted nothing more than to take Syd back to my place and fuck her all night long.

I could never get enough.

"So," Sydney said as she worked her shirt over her head. "Where does this leave us, Zack?"

I slid my shirt over my chest and walked toward her, capturing her in my arms.

"It leaves us right where we want to be. I won't ask to move in, yet."

She let out a nervous laugh, and I knew she was struggling with this. Hell, I was too, a thousand things running through my mind as to how this could go wrong. We were two different people in two different worlds, and no amount of love was going to catch that.

But as I looked down at her, capturing her lips with mine, I knew I was willing to try.

I wasn't giving her up again.

***

The rag tasted like oil and day-old body sweat, numbing her tongue and making her want to gag. She had attempted to work on the rag, to get it to loosen so she could get it out of her mouth, but so far the knot hadn't budged.

Neither had the ones at her hands or her feet, cutting into her skin and rubbing it raw. Hayley Travis let out a sound of frustration, not allowing the tears to fall. She was done crying.

She was a Travis, and Travis's didn't cry.

The door opened, and the light flickered overhead, momentarily blinding her. She didn't know how long she had been in the building, how many hours had gone by. Probably more like days. Ever since she had been pulled out of her car and thrown into the dirty van that had brought her here, her sense of time had been off.

That, and the building had no windows. It was just a concrete shed, cool inside from the insulated bricks. Twice a day she was untied and blindfolded, taken to a bathroom where she was allowed to do her business. The first day she had attempted to find a weapon, but unless she was going to tear the toilet out there was nothing to help her.

She was by herself.

"How are you today?"

Hayley's eyes focused on the face, something familiar about him. He was one of her father's bikers; which one, she didn't know. She imagined that, if he removed his shirt, she would see the tattoo of the Devil's Horsemen, which was far more concerning to her than anything else.

Her father was being betrayed.

"Oh, I guess you can't speak right now. Well that's alright. I imagine you haven't found anything exciting in this building to entertain yourself with."

She glared at him, not even uttering a word behind the rag. She had only tried once to fight back, rewarded with a bruise on her jaw and pain for hours.

He lowered himself in front of her, his hand touching her knee, and she flinched against his touch. A thousand things had run through her mind of what he might do to her, rape being one of them.

But today was the first day he had touched her.

"Don't worry," he chuckled, seeing her revulsion. "As much as I would love to fuck you until you submitted to me, that isn't the plan. I'll let you in a little secret, Hayley. My plan is to ruin your father. You are just my insurance that he will go down the wrong path and never expect that one of his own would be the person that would turn against him."

He removed his hand and ran them both through his graying hair.

"You see, I want to be the leader of the DHMC. They have grown soft under your father's rein, and I want us to be the premier club in this shit-hole town. He's holding us back from our potential, and when the cartel kills him I will assume the power and control of the club. Then we will turn into the Devils that we are named after."

Hayley felt like vomiting. Her father was no angel, but he didn't like for the club to be involved in anything illegal or immoral. She had heard things about the cartel, what they did to women and those that they sold into sex slavery. Her father had stayed away from them, not wanting to start a war, but this dude was going to force his hand.

All because he thought the cartel had her.

She wanted to scream and cry, kick at him, and make him feel some of this pain in her chest, but she forced herself to sit there, glaring at him. He would die, and she would make sure that her face was the last thing he saw as she drove the knife into his black heart.

After all, she was a Travis.

Chapter Thirteen
Sydney

I fidgeted as I sat in the chief's office, waiting for him to arrive. I knew why he had called me to the office, the summons coming via text message, and while I was nervous about the encounter, I knew I hadn't been in the wrong.

Sighing, I leaned back in one of the chairs, my thoughts on the night before. Oh, how I should be embarrassed that I'd had sex in a field!

With Zack.

And fully enjoyed it.

This was clearly going to complicate things between us, my feelings stuck between this being reality and whether I was destined for another heartbreak. He had said many things to me last night, hinting that he had been in love with me before my world blew up and I was left alone. He didn't want that to happen again.

But could we co-exist the way our lives were now? I was a cop. He was, by all accounts, a criminal. We weren't meant to be together.

I rubbed a hand over my face, my mind drifting back to the previous night. Something had made us find our way to each other again. The sex last night… it had been incredible, however brief it had been. I had never felt so alive, so complete, as I had with Zack. He knew me inside and out, and though the years had separated us, I felt like some of those feelings, some of those emotions were still there.

And knowing that he had my initials tattooed on his chest… That was… well, I couldn't even describe that. It meant he hadn't forgotten me. It meant he hadn't abandoned me.

It meant I meant something to him, something very important.

And when I had dropped him off at the clubhouse, I hadn't wanted to leave. On the outside, we were still cop and biker to everyone that was looking.

But in that one brief moment, we were just Sydney and Zack again, two oddballs that should have never experienced anything together like we had, either now or then. I still felt like that young girl riding in his truck, experiencing my first taste at love with a guy I should have known better than to be with. Was it the same for Zack? He had told me yes, but given our history, I was somewhat afraid to believe him.

What if he broke my heart again?

I wouldn't be able to stay. I had already been embarrassed once before, but for it to happen a second time…? I would either have to leave or he would end up dead, his body buried where no one would ever find it.

I couldn't go through that again.

"You idiot," I whispered to myself, glancing around to make sure no one was watching me.

I shouldn't have slept with Zack. I shouldn't have gone down that path, opening my heart to him while knowing what we were dealing with right now. This wasn't high school anymore. This wasn't just Zack and Syd. This was real life, and we both had responsibilities that could not be avoided just because we wanted to continue our relationship.

Oh, why did this have to be so complicated?

"Warren."

I jumped to my feet as the chief entered, an envelope in his hand. I had fully expected to see the station's lawyer follow him, but there was no one else behind him as he shut the door, motioning for me to sit down.

I did so, swallowing my emotions as he took his position behind his desk, placing the envelope on its scarred surface. For a moment he just looked at me, assessing me under his bushy eyebrows with a hard stare that made me want to crawl into my body and hide from him. When he had summoned me that morning, I knew I would be grilled about my involvement in the shooting the day before. I hadn't reported that I had fired my weapon, but there was a nagging feeling inside that made me think that was what I was there for.

After all, I had been the one to make the anonymous call about the body in the desert.

"Sydney," he started, folding his hands in front of him. "You know I why I hired you on?"

I shook my head.

"I do not, sir."

"Because you were willing to face your demons straight on," he answered roughly. "I doubt there would be many people that would come back to Cibolo after what you went through, to help the people that ridiculed you. That takes some balls, and I knew you were going to be good for this department."

"T-thank you sir," I stammered, surprised.

Since my return, we hadn't talked much about my past, me not wanting to focus on the bad things that had happened here. I had wanted to make a difference in my hometown. Well, and a tiny piece of me had wanted to show those that had turned their back on me that I was much more than what they had thought. I wasn't the girl they had labeled as a 'biker slut' or 'whore', the one they had laughed about when I walked down the street, the one that had endured a miserable month of her senior year only because I refused to go away and hide from them.

"However," he continued, tapping his fingers on the desk. "I think we might have a problem, Warren."

Back to the last name again. This couldn't be good.

"What is that, sir?"

"Why are you working with Hale?"

I blew out a breath, choosing my words carefully. It had only been a matter of time before someone found out, and up until last night it was going to be easy to defend my choice.

Now, shit, there were emotions involved.

"I… he was assigned to the case by Grant Travis," I said truthfully, looking the police chief in the eye. "We were fighting each other. I thought it would make more sense to collaborate together to reach the same goal."

The chief eyed me.

"Did that include kidnapping one Muertos and killing another?"

I remained silent, finding that it was easier to not defend what he already knew.

And honestly, I had forgotten all about the tied-up Muertos in the police warehouse.

"I didn't harm him sir."

"Didn't harm him? Didn't harm him! You kidnapped him and left him tied to a chair, Warren! You are lucky he can't talk any more or your ass would be grass."

Stunned, I looked at him.

"W-what?"

"He's dead," the chief said flatly, pushing the manila envelope toward me. "SWAT found him when they went to retrieve some equipment."

My hands shook slightly as I picked up the envelope and opened the flap, dumping out the pictures in my hand. The dead Muertos stared up at me, a perfectly round hole in the center of his forehead. When I had seen him last, he was cursing and bucking against the chair.

He wasn't dead.

I looked up at Chief Turner, not bothering to hide my shock.

"He was alive last time I saw him."

"I know," the chief said, leaning back in his chair. "The bullet doesn't match your gun, Warren. I had them check, discreetly of course."

I swallowed hard. If it wasn't my gun, then whose was it?

"What do you know about the Devil's Horsemen, Warren?"

"Everything you have told me, and what I've read of course," I answered truthfully.

I had done a great deal of research on the biker gang, especially since I knew that Zack was a part of them.

That was before last night.

"They are at war with the cartel," the chief explained. "Turf wars are popping up everywhere in this town. I know you were with Hale. Did it ever occur to you that he might be looking for a way to get even with the cartel?"

I didn't say anything, curling my hand into a fist.

No, it hadn't crossed my mind. Zack was looking for Hayley. Our past had brought us together. He didn't have a hidden agenda.

Right?

"I'm going to give you a piece of advice," the chief said softly. "You can't trust any of them Sydney. They had their own agendas, their own ways of doing things, long before you or Hale got involved. The Horsemen thrive on getting their hands dirty with the cartel, and I can promise you this incident won't go unnoticed."

"Chief, I don't think Zack did this," I finally forced out.

I knew Zack. He would never resort to killing a man like this, at point blank range. Sure, he had pulled his gun out yesterday, but we were both under fire. He was protecting himself and me.

The chief eyed me.

"Did you take him to the interrogation?"

"Yes," I said softly.

I had given him that location. He knew where the Muertos was and knew that someone would find him. He had followed me in and out the door, watching me as I punched into the key pad.

Oh, God! What if Zack had done this?

Chief Turner reached into his drawer and pulled out a thick file, pushing it toward me.

"Go home. I'm not pulling you from the case because I don't want Amy Travis breathing down my neck, but I am going to be watching you closely. One wrong move, Warren, and I will step in."

"Thank you, sir," I breathed, grateful that I wasn't going to be yanked because of my stupidity.

I was, however, going to have a talk with my 'partner'.

"And read this," he continued, tapping on the file. "I think you need to see what you are dealing with."

I scooped it up and held it close to my chest as I stood.

"I won't let you down again, sir."

"Watch your ass, Sydney," he said as I made my way toward the door. "Don't let your past get in the way of your good common sense."

I didn't respond as I headed out of the station and to my jeep, hating the fact that he'd had to tell me that. I had already let my past right back into my life, screwing around with my job and nearly getting me yanked from a case in the process.

That was not going to happen again.

After picking up some lunch, I went home, grabbing the file from the passenger seat along with my food. My cell phone had been quiet all morning, and I wondered how long it was going to be until Zack contacted me.

If he contacted me.

"You're being ridiculous," I muttered as I flopped on my couch, the file in my lap.

Of course, he was going to call. He wasn't the same person as before.

But as I opened the file, I realized what the chief had given me. It was Zack's file, much thicker than I had imagined it would be. There was intel from undercover cops on his movements in the past, shortly after I'd left. Beatings, break-ins, public intoxication were just a few of the notable reasons he had gotten put into jail for a day or two.

My food forgotten, I read through some of the reports, my stomach churning. While he had no murders tied to him, he had been pulled into the interrogation room many times over the past few years, asked about their rift with the cartel. His comments had been candid and not even close to what the investigators needed, but they had tried. I could imagine Zack sitting in the chair as he had that day with me, that cocky grin on his face, knowing he wouldn't get nailed with anything as long as they had their legal counsel.

Leaning back on the couch, I fought the emotions that were swirling around in my body. The chief was right. I had allowed my judgement to be clouded by Zack, throwing out my police training, and given him a cartel member on a silver platter. If Zack hadn't pulled that trigger, that didn't mean that someone else hadn't got the information from him to make it happen.

That was where his loyalty lay. It didn't with me. If it had, we would never have broken up.

I closed the file and pushed it aside, rubbing a hand over my face. All my euphoric feelings from before were gone. Instead, dread was in its place. Zack couldn't have killed that informant. I would know if he had done it, right?

Well there was only one way to find out. I would have to ask him, confront him with the evidence and see if he would tell me the truth. I wanted to say that I would recognize it if he was lying but wasn't so sure about that either.

What a mess I had gotten myself in!

Reaching for my phone, I fired off a text to him, with a meeting place in an hour. I didn't want him over here at my house, my resolve too weak after the previous night, and I sure as hell didn't want to be at the clubhouse when I confronted him.

No telling what might happen then.

I got back a thumbs up, and I stood, tucking the phone in my back pocket. I was still on Hayley's case and I owed Amy Travis an update.

***

"So, you are telling me that she wasn't with the cartel?"

I shook my head, gripping the coffee cup in my hand.

"The lead didn't pan out. I'm not sure who has her, but it wasn't that guy."

Amy blew out a breath, her expression one of sadness and concern. We sat at the only coffee house in Cibolo. Honestly, though: I had tasted better coffee!

"Great, just fucking great. I'm sick and tired of not knowing where she is at."

I nodded sympathetically.

"I know it's tough. But I will find her, I swear it."

She looked at me, a peculiar look on her face.

"You know, I'm surprised by you, Sydney. You clearly are not the girl that this stupid town branded a whore."

My cheeks flushed. If she'd only known what I had done the night before, she might have a different opinion.

Amy leaned forward, a smirk on her face.

"I would dearly like to know how you bagged Zack Hale though. I saw you dropping him off last night. That look he gave you… well, I haven't seen him look at anyone like that before."

"That's in the past," I forced out, draining the rest of my coffee.

And it would be if he was the one responsible for this cartel member's death. As much as I loved him, I had a duty to this town as well. I couldn't, and wouldn't, turn a blind eye to murder.

But first, I had to confront him about it.

Chapter Fourteen
Zack

I knew something was wrong the minute she stepped out of her jeep.

Leaning against my truck, I watched as Sydney walked toward me, her brisk pace sending all kinds of warning bells off in my head. This was not the woman who had smiled at me with love in her eyes the previous night.

This was a woman on a mission.

Which was probably why we were meeting out here at the old railroad yard, far away from any prying eyes. I didn't imagine she was looking for afternoon sex.

"Hey," I said as she came up to me.

"Hey," she said, not meeting my eyes. "I have to ask you something, Zack, and I need for you to be completely honest about it. I-I… this partnership depends on your answer."

I shrugged a shoulder.

"Fire away."

She looked up and I was surprised to see the concern in her depths. What the hell had happened between last night and right now?

"Did you…? God I can't even say it."

I gritted my teeth, my mind racing with possibilities of what she could be asking. If it was anything about the inner workings of the club, I couldn't answer. But… hell, anything else was on the table. I would even tell her how many women, if she really wanted to know, that I'd had my fun, never expecting to see them again.

But it didn't mean I hadn't dreamed of her, keeping my damn emotions out of any fuck I had encountered after she had left Cibolo. There was only one person that held my heart, and she looked scared to death at the moment.

"Just lay it out, Syd."

She blew out a breath.

"Fine, you are right. Did you kill that informant from yesterday?"

A bark of laughter escaped me before I could control it.

"Are you fucking serious?"

Sydney nodded.

"I am. He's dead and I just spent half the morning defending my actions yesterday. Did you kill him, Zack?"

I didn't know whether to be flattered or pissed off at her.

"What do you think, Syd?" I asked darkly, crossing my arms over my chest.

She stared at me.

"I honestly don't know Zack."

Her words were not a surprise to me. I was an outlaw, a biker, and she was a cop. It was her nature to accuse the person that was closest to her. I had thought after last night... well, maybe not.

"Are you going to arrest me?"

Sydney let out a laugh.

"How can I?"

"Are you going to force me off the case?"

She shook her head slowly.

"No, no, I'm not. But if you even remotely step out of line, Zack, I will not hesitate to arrest you."

"Fair enough," I answered roughly, hating the fact that we were back to square one with our reunion.

She didn't trust me. I couldn't change who I was or the life I was leading as an adult.

"I can't change who I am. Syd."

She blew out a breath.

"I-I know that. Let's just try to co-exist until we get this case solved."

I stepped forward, unable to help myself. Her throat bobbed as I reached down with my hand and brushed it over her cheek. I had done nothing but think about her since the moment she had dropped me off the previous night, anticipating that we would pick up where we'd left off for multiple rounds in my bed.

But now… hell, this changed everything.

"We are going to have to talk eventually, Syd."

She seemed to lean into my touch before clearing her throat and stepping away, out of my reach.

"Let's just focus on the case right now."

Alright, I could do that.

"I got some news."

Her eyes lit up.

"You do?"

I nodded.

"There's been reports that Hayley's card has been used outside of town."

"How?" she started before waving a hand. "Never mind. Let's go then."

I motioned toward my truck.

"Let me drive."

Sydney gave a shrug and I grinned.

Score one for me.

***

We ended up out on the outskirts of Cibolo, near a plaza full of shops. I pulled into the gas station and cut the engine. Sydney climbed out and I followed her, allowing her to take the lead. She was the cop, and I had to remember that.

For now.

We walked into the gas station and approached the clerk, who was eyeing us with some concern.

"I'm looking for your manager," Sydney stated. "I need some information."

The clerk shrugged.

"I've been told to not give out anything, else you got a warrant. You got one?"

Sydney looked as if she wanted to jump across the counter.

"A woman's life is in danger."

"Sorry," the clerk said, going back to tapping on her cell phone.

"Come on," I said, touching her shoulder. "We can get it by other means."

Sydney let out a frustrated breath as we stalked outside.

"I can't believe this. I will never get a warrant on a hunch."

I looked at the parking lot.

"You don't have to."

Sydney followed my gaze before breaking into a dead run. Hayley's car was not hard to spot, parked in front of a Chinese restaurant. I would know that powder blue color anywhere, the number of times it had been parked in front of the clubhouse.

Sydney reached the car first and tried the door handle, finding it open. I frowned as I saw the specks of blood on the driver seat, felt a sickening feeling in the pit of my stomach.

Shit. Not what anyone wanted to find.

"I have to call this in," Sydney said as she looked up at me. "If you want to do the same."

I shook my head.

"No. I want to tell him in person."

***

An hour later, Sydney and I walked into the clubhouse, ignoring everyone who stared at us as we passed. I had one thing on my mind, and no one was going to stop me from doing this. I led Sydney straight to Grant's office, where the leader was seated behind his desk, joined by the Vice President of the DHMC, Grayson Barnes. Grayson was the man who had shown me the ropes of the club, my mentor, as I learned the ways of the Horsemen. He had even gone as far as to sponsor me at his home for a while, until I could get enough funds to support myself.

"Zack," Grayson said, eyeing Sydney. "What are you doing here?"

I ran a hand through my hair, hoping that Sydney would stick to our plan. On the ride over, I had asked her to let me tell Grant about the car instead of finding out from the police. He had appointed me to find his daughter, and I wanted to be the one to deliver the news.

"We found Hayley's car."

Grant dropped the pen he was holding, standing behind his desk. He was visibly shaken, the look on his face a mixture of instant concern and a hint of fear.

"Where."

I told him the location. "The cops are crawling all over it right now."

"Because of you," Grant said to Sydney, narrowing his gaze. "Why the hell did you allow that to happen?"

"I know you don't like the cops involved," she replied evenly.

I was amazed at how she could keep her cool in front of him, a hint of pride flowing through my veins at her expression. She was a damn good cop.

"But I had to involve them. They can process the car and maybe pull some evidence."

Grant looked over at me, blowing out a breath.

"Was there… was there anything in it?"

I glanced at Sydney, who gave me a small nod to share what we had seen.

"There were small amounts of blood in the driver seat. I can't tell you if it's hers or not."

"Shit," Grant swore, falling back in his seat. "She's dead."

"Now Grant," Grayson said softly, laying a hand on his friend's shoulder. "Let's not jump to conclusions. It doesn't mean shit."

"He's right," Sydney interjected. "Let us process the car."

I watched as Grayson eyed Sydney, clearly not happy she was here or butting into the conversation. He wouldn't say anything, probably already aware that Amy had reached out for Syd's help, but he didn't like it.

I didn't like the way that made me feel.

"Double the efforts," Grant finally said, waving a hand at us. "I don't want any fucking stone unturned! I want Hayley's name on everyone's lips and the merest hint of where she might be reported to me immediately."

"I heard something," Grayson said softly. "I was going to tell you before we were rudely interrupted."

"What?" Grant said coldly. "What did you find out?"

I bristled. I didn't know that Grayson was looking into the disappearance as well. I had thought that was a job specifically assigned to me.

Grayson gave me a look before his eyes moved to Sydney.

"Spit it out," Grant demanded, impatient. "I'm waiting."

"The cartel," Grayson said carefully. "They have her."

Well that wasn't anything new.

"No shit," Grant swore.

Grayson's expression grew angry.

"They are holding her somewhere close. It's a trap and they are hoping that you will come get her, so they can take their shot."

Grant's laugh was hollow.

"That's never going to fucking happen. Where is this place?"

"Yeah where is it?" Sydney added, crossing her arms over her chest. "Give us something useful."

Grayson's eyes grew dark as he looked at Sydney, and I wanted to bash his face in for that look he was given her.

"Fuck off, cop. You shouldn't even be here."

"Just fucking tell us," Grant interrupted. "Before I blow your head off."

"I don't know," Grayson spit out. "But I know a kid. He knows exactly where she is."

"Tell me his name," I said softly, my voice laced with steel.

I was tired of the games. I wanted to find Hayley and then sit down with Sydney, tell her that I did not shoot that gringo, and prove to her that I was more than just the biker she thought me to be.

"Jason," Grayson said after a moment. "He's at the bar on Southside. It's where he does trafficking of drugs and shit for the cartel. If anyone knows, it would be him."

"Let's go," Sydney said, turning her back to the two men as she caught my eye. "Time is wasting."

"Find my fucking daughter," Grant called after us as we exited the office, walking back through the clubhouse.

Hell, I wanted to find Hayley, so I could end this.

"I'll drive," Sydney said as we walked to the truck.

I chuckled, giving her the eye as she reached out her hand for the keys.

"Are you serious?"

She pursed her lips.

"I'm not in the mood Zack. Give me the keys."

"It's my fucking truck."

"Fine," she stated, dropping her hand. "Then take me back to my jeep and I will go by myself."

I took a step toward her, pissed off that she was treating this like nothing had happened between us.

"I thought we were going to do this together."

She wouldn't look at me.

"I… I can't trust you Zack. Maybe you should back out and let the professionals handle this."

I stared at her for a moment before grabbing her arm, ignoring her yelps as I walked over to the line of bikes that were in front of the clubhouse. Mine sat where I had left it.

"Get the hell on the bike Syd."

She looked at me incredulously.

"What?"

"We are taking the bike," I said, pulling out the small key.

"We are most certainly not taking the bike," she answered as I slid the key into the ignition.

With a frustrated sigh, I trapped her against the bike, leaning in so she could see my eyes clearly.

"We are taking the bike. I'm tired of fucking around with you and this pulling rank shit. It's time for me to do it my way, and if you want any piece of this, you will get on the bike."

Her eyes narrowed, and I knew I had caught her attention. She was beyond pissed. Hell, she was turning me on with that look.

"I don't like being bossed around."

"I know," I said with a hollow chuckle. I knew that all too well. "Get on the bike. I won't say it again."

She looked over at the bike and, with a curse, slung her leg over. I did the same, ignoring her touch as she grabbed at my waist immediately. I knew that Syd hated to ride motorcycles. In fact, she was scared to death of them, but I guess the thought of being left in the dust had gotten her on mine.

Cranking the engine, I let the bike run for a second, feeling her fingers grip my belt buckle tightly. I wanted to comfort her, but something in me held back. She thought I had shot someone, killed him, that could be directly tied back to her. She must have gotten an earful from her chief this morning. That was the only thing that would explain her odd behavior.

And the fact that she was believing him over me. Was this a red flag that we might not be able to co-exist after all was said and done? I wanted Sydney and had no thoughts of letting her go this time, but there was this big rift between us. I wouldn't ask her to give up the force, and she was not the type of person to make me give up the club.

So where did that leave us? I was scared to ask. I couldn't lose her again, not after the previous night. There was more to this than just having Sydney in my bed. There were feelings, feelings that hadn't gone away from the first go-round, that were tied up in this mess as well. No matter what she thought of me, I knew she cared about me.

"Are we going to go?" Sydney shouted into my ear.

I shook out of my thoughts and backed the bike out of the tight spot, positioning it in the right direction.

"Hold on!" I yelled before I gunned it down the highway.

Her hands tightened on me, but I forced myself to think of other things, like finding Hayley. Sydney, and whatever was going on with us, would have to take a back seat for now. I needed to find Grant's daughter and soon. If the cartel really had her, every hour she was in their hands was another hour that they could torture her. I wouldn't put it past them either.

So, this kid, this informant, better have some shit for me today. I was starting to lose my patience.

Chapter Fifteen
Sydney

I hated motorcycles.

My teeth chattered against each other, and there were tears in my eyes from the tearing wind, as Zack tore down the highway, far faster than he should. My hands were starting to ache from the death grip I had on him, but I knew it was hopeless to try and get him to slow down. I was terrified that he would hit a bump and I would go flying off the back of the bike, or that when he turned I would fall off. Each scenario ended with me on the asphalt, and I didn't like it.

That, and my life was in his hands. One wrong move and he could end it for us both, and after today I didn't know if I should trust him completely.

Forcing myself not to press my face into his shirt, I thought about the one and only other time I had ridden a motorcycle with Zack.

***

I hurried down the sidewalk, looking back over my shoulder to make sure that my parents weren't watching me from the window. This was the third time this week I had told them I was going to the library, under the impression that I needed to cram for my finals.

But in reality, I was meeting Zack yet again. I wasn't the type to lie to my parents, but the mere thought of seeing him had butterflies dancing in my stomach. After the last few weeks, I was falling in love with him and it was a scary feeling. At some point, I would have to come clean to my parents about him and hope that they would understand.

I wasn't quite sure how they would take him.

Turning the corner, I skidded to a stop. Instead of the truck I was used to seeing, Zack was leaning against a gleaming motorcycle.

"Hey babe."

"What's that?" I asked instead as I approached.

"It's my bike," he said casually, his grin causing my heart to flip over in my chest. "I thought you might like to go for a spin."

My inner self sighed as I took in his handsome form, the way he wore a t-shirt and jeans like they were a second skin. I knew what that body looked like under his clothes, though we had yet to actually do the deed. I knew it wouldn't be long. I had held him off for a month or more, but a guy like Zack... he wasn't going to wait around forever for me to get over the fact that I would be losing my virginity.

I had thought about it far more lately than I should.

But back to the present. There was a motorcycle, and Zack wanted me to ride it with him.

"I-I can't do that."

His grin faded, and he pushed away from the bike.

"Why not?"

I stared at the death trap.

"Do you know how many people die each day on these things? There's nothing to keep you from eating the road... or worse!"

His grin re-appeared, and he took my face in his hands, his skin warm against mine. I sighed in happiness as he brushed his lips over mine, a featherlight kiss that did nothing but rev up my body for what was to come later.

"Come on Syd. You know I would never let anything happen to you. I'm a damn good driver with this thing, and I won't do anything stupid, I swear."

"I know," I said, searching his eyes. It was hard to believe that he was all mine. "B-but I can't Zack. I'm sorry."

He stepped back, dropping his hands.

"I tell you what. Let me take you just around the block. If you hate it, I will go get my truck and I will never ask you do this again."

I bit my lip, staring at the gleaming chrome.

"Are you sure you won't be mad if I don't like it?"

He shook his head, reaching for the helmet that was hanging from the handle.

"Of course not. I just want to be with you, Syd."

***

The bike slowed, and I shook out of the memory. True to his statement, he had taken me around the block, me beating on his back to take me back about one hundred yards into the ride. I had gotten off of his bike, swearing I would never do it again.

Yet here I was.

I couldn't let him leave me, though. If this was truly a good lead, we could crack this case today. This could all be over.

Zack pulled into a parking lot and parked the bike, cutting the engine.

"See? That wasn't so bad."

I forced myself to peel my arms from around him.

"You really think I liked that?"

He chuckled, and I wanted to press my cheek to his strong back to feel it against my skin.

"No, but a man can always dream."

I snorted and climbed off the bike, my legs still vibrating from the engine.

"I'm just glad it's over."

"You still have to get back, Syd."

"I'll call a cab."

He shook his head and swung his long leg over the bike, standing before me. There was a grin on his face, and I desperately tried to fight returning it with one of my own. Inside I was torn up about the fact that he could be the man who had killed that Muertos. He hadn't denied it, and I was scared for him. This was Zack, the guy I had loved more than anything in this entire world at one time. I shouldn't even be questioning him for the killing, yet there was a nagging doubt that he could be that person. He wasn't that man any longer. He was a Horseman, under the thumb of Grant Travis.

I had no bearing on him, even after last night.

A small piece of my heart withered and died as I turned from him, pretending to inspect the building before us.

"Are you sure this is the right place?"

"Yeah," he said, walking past me. "Come on. Don't say a word in here about you being a cop, Syd. I mean it."

I wasn't planning on it unless the situation warranted it.

I followed Zack toward the concrete building, noting the flashing lights that advertised the beer and liquors they served. I would give my right arm for a stiff drink right now, something to take the edge off and make me forget for a while.

After this case was solved, I was going on vacation. Especially if Zack was found to be part of that murder. I wouldn't be able to deal with it.

The interior smelled of stale smoke and body odor, only a few people inside the dimly lit bar. There was some sort of soccer game on the TV behind the bar, with a tired-looking bartender wiping out his glasses in front of it. Zack walked right up to the bar, not even glancing at the rest of his surroundings.

"Where's Jason?"

I tapped my fingers against my arm as I surveyed our surroundings for us, noting the exits and the number of people inside. The odds were in our favor.

A tall, skinny guy in the back stood, and I knew immediately that it was Jason.

"Got him," I said under my breath as I started toward the back.

We locked eyes and he ran for the exit door, slamming into it and disappearing.

I swore and took off running, slamming into the door as well and finding myself outside. Not waiting for Zack, I drew my gun and crept around the building. The corner was a large blind spot, and if I wasn't careful, I could be walking into a trap.

Easing alongside the building, I took in a breath and walked out, my gun out in front of me. Zack was there, with Jason jacked up against the building. The kid's feet were dangling several feet in the air and I holstered my gun. There was an upside to having a muscle with me.

"Where's Hayley Travis?" he growled as the kid squirmed against his hold. "Your life depends on your answers."

"I-I don't know!" Jason wailed, clawing at Zack's hands around his neck. "You're hurting me!"

"Good," Zack replied, his eyes on the informant. "Tell me what I need to know, and I might let you go."

"Zack," I warned as Jason's face turned red.

Zack ignored me and before I knew it, he was slamming Jason against the wall, the kid's head bouncing violently on the concrete brick.

"Tell me!" he shouted, as blood started to appear on the whitewashed wall behind Jason.

"Zack!" I shouted, laying a hand on his arm. "Let him go."

"Fuck off," Zack growled not looking at me and doing it again, Jason barely making a sound this time.

I was stunned. There was a wild look about him, reminding me of the last time I had seen him like this. Pulling my gun, I pointed it at his head, my heart tearing in two.

"You have to let him go, Zack."

"Did you just pull a gun on me Syd?" he asked in a low voice.

"I did," I said, my hand not shaking surprisingly. "Now let him go."

"I… you need to watch your own back," Jason wheezed, his voice cracking. "Money will turn anyone, man."

I thought over Jason's words. Could there be a traitor in DHMC? It would make sense.

But I couldn't think about that right now. My hand started to cramp, but I held the gun tight. I wasn't going to shoot him, nor did I think I could ever shoot Zack. But if I had to pull rank on him, I would.

"Come on, let him go."

Zack let out a frustrated sound and dropped the kid, who crumpled to the ground with a groan. I lowered my weapon immediately, placing it back in the holster.

But when Zack turned toward me, I didn't recognize him. A shiver of fear snaked down my spine as I saw the wild look in his eyes, the anger that was radiating off him.

"Zack," I said softly, showing him my hands. "Let's go."

"Shit man! I think you broke my throat!"

Zack turned back to the kid, kicking him hard in the ribs.

"Tell me something useful and I might not kill you."

"Zack," I warned. "Leave him alone."

"You wanted information, right?" he sneered, reaching for the kid. "We need to know, Sydney."

I watched helplessly as he landed a few punches, the kid whimpering and not attempting to block Zack's shots. I didn't know what to do.

"S-she's at the auto shop," the kid choked out, spitting out blood at Zack's feet. "Damn man, you broke a rib!"

I reached out and gripped Zack's arm as he attempted to go for him again, my heart pounding in my chest. This was a solid lead.

"Come on Zack, let's go."

Zack looked at me and, for a moment, I was scared at what I saw reflected in his eyes. This was not the loving Zack at all.

***

Zack's hand curled around mine as we walked out of the movie theater. The movie had sucked, but just being near him had been enough for me. I loved spending time with my complete polar opposite, the tender way he treated me when it was just the two of us. He made me feel like I was the most beautiful girl in the world, and I felt a measure of pride when others saw us together, including the other girls in town. I could see it in their eyes, that they wanted him, and I had him.

It was unbelievable.

"What are you smiling about?"

I looked up to find him grinning down at me.

"I'm just happy, that's all."

"Good," he said as we rounded the corner, where he had parked the truck. "Because that movie blew ass."

I laughed, my laughter dying as I saw the truck. There was a guy there, lounging against it as if he had all the time in the world.

"What the fuck man?" Zack shouted, letting go of my hand. "Get the hell off my truck!"

The man grinned, flicking his cigarette onto the sidewalk.

"I've been waiting for you, Hale. We have a score to settle."

"You're damn right we do," Zack answered, peeling off his jacket.

I watched, dumbfounded as Zack landed a punch, looking excited to be doing so. I was rooted on the spot, torn between running for help and running toward Zack to get him to stop.

Zack landed a few more punches, and the man fell to the ground, where he picked up kicking as well as punching the man, who was now barely fighting back.

"Zack!" I shouted, running over. "Stop!"

It was like he couldn't hear me at all. I reached in and grabbed at his arm, succeeding in getting him to stop.

"Stop! You're going to kill him!"

Zack pushed away from me, his eyes wild, and for the first time I was scared of him.

"Don't ever fucking touch me while I'm kicking someone's ass, Syd," he growled, shoving his bleeding knuckles through his hair. "Don't interfere."

I bit my lip, angry tears springing to my eyes.

"This isn't you."

He smiled grimly.

"This is me."

I gave a look at the man on the ground, broken and bleeding, and turned away, walking quickly back to the theatre.

This was not Zack, not my Zack.

***

I shook out of the memory, dropping my hand on his arm as I remembered his warnings from way back when.

"Come on," I tried again. "We have to go."

Some of the wildness died in his eyes, and he stepped back, not apologizing as he moved past me, rounding the corner of the building. I took one look at the bleeding kid, knowing I should call in some medical for him. But if I did, that would lead to questions I wasn't ready to answer.

"Go inside," I told him. "Get some help."

He stared at me, but I managed to get a small nod from him before I followed Zack's path, finding him already firing up the bike. Wordlessly, I climbed on the death trap again, gripping the back of his pants this time instead of wrapping my arms around his waist.

That memory had come out of nowhere, triggered by the fight, and I could remember even then the despair I had felt as I had gotten a ride home. The silence the next few days had nearly killed me, but he had been the first to apologize. I had forgiven him, and until now I had never seen him fight anyone else, though I was sure he had done it without me around. That was part of who he was, the fighter in him, either with his father or with the club.

What was I going to do?

Chapter Sixteen
Zack

I had lost control.

I gripped the handles tighter as I tore down the highway, fully aware that Sydney was gripping the back of my pants as if I was going to throw her off.

I would die before I let that happen.

But after what she had just witnessed, no doubt she was trying to figure out what to do about it. I had lost control, which was something rare for me nowadays. Sure, I still got into scrapes and fights, but never to the point where I wanted to kill someone. The informant had been just a kid, but I was tired of the jerking around. I wanted to take Syd and go find a place to hole up in, escape this damn reality that brought out the worst in me.

Sydney had pulled a gun on me. I still couldn't believe it. Her arm had been steady enough to pull the trigger, though the look in her eyes… it had been devastating. I didn't know if she would shoot me or not.

And now there might be a traitor in our midst. What the hell was that about? The Horsemen were supposed to be brothers, looking out for each other when no one else would. Not kidnapping the leader's daughter.

No, the informant had to have that information wrong. Everyone was as loyal as fuck in that clubhouse.

I turned the bike to the right and pulled over, shutting off the engine.

"What are you doing?" Sydney asked as I climbed off, raking my hands through my hair.

"I'm getting my shit together," I answered hoarsely, my nerves on edge.

I was fucking falling apart on the inside, partly because of her.

She tucked her hair behind her ears, looking past me.

"What do you think about this traitor?"

I blew out a breath.

"That can't possibly be true. No one would fucking cross Grant."

"Why?" she asked with a little laugh. "Because he's some god in that clubhouse? He's just a man, like everyone else, in a very high position."

"Because…" I bit out. "We are a family, unlike your little police station."

She looked at me and I saw the fire burning in her eyes.

"What does that mean?"

"Whatever you want it to," I muttered, rubbing my face. "They don't give a shit about anything else but putting us under the microscope. That's why your precious chief let you work with me. So, he could have an inside scoop on what we do."

Her mouth opened.

"You're not serious."

I crossed my arms over my chest.

"Then tell me why, Sydney."

She started at me, still straddling the bike. There could have been a time I would be turned on by the sight, but right now I was pissed at her, the world, this shit we were in.

"I can't believe you are saying that to me," she finally said. "I wasn't the one losing my cool back there."

"You pulled a fucking gun on me," I forced out. "Me Syd, not anyone else. What am I supposed to think?"

"You almost killed him!" she shouted back. "If I hadn't interfered."

"We wouldn't have gotten anything!" I shouted, throwing up my hands. "Sometimes you got to bend the rules. Not everything fits into your perfect little world, Syd."

She let out a bitter laugh.

"*My* perfect world? Are you forgetting who you are talking to?"

I stared at her, some of my anger draining as I saw the hurt in her eyes. She was right. She hadn't had the perfect world. Neither had I. But I had wanted to give it to her. Back then, I hadn't known how I was going to do so, but I had wanted to.

Sydney broke her gaze, swallowing hard.

"Listen, I don't want to fight with you. We need to find Hayley, so we can get out of this mess."

"Agreed," I answered. "I need to call this into Grant."

"No," Sydney said quickly as I reached for my phone "You can't do that."

I arched a brow. The hell I couldn't. If the cartel was involved, we would need backup. The last time had been too close of a call for us, for Sydney, and I wanted nothing like that to happen again.

"Why not?"

She looked down at the bike.

"What if the kid was right? Wouldn't that be tipping off the mole?"

"There is no mole," I said angrily. "He was lying."

She looked up, concern written all over her face.

"But what if he wasn't?"

I didn't want to think about that. To have someone on the inside attempting to blow up the clubhouse… it was unthinkable. I had given up everything, including the woman before me, to be part of that brotherhood.

I knew I wasn't the only one.

Sydney pulled out her cell and I frowned.

"What are you doing?"

"Letting Roger know what's going on," she answered, not looking up. "About Hayley, nothing else."

I knew she had a different reason for doing so. It was her job. I wanted to warn the club because it was my duty. While we thought we were the same, we were the complete opposites. I had a loyalty, she had a job to protect. Though she hadn't said anything, I felt as if she had gone through hell today to even get to this point.

So, I let it go. I trusted Syd. She might have some questions about me, but I knew her. I knew the girl that had stolen my fucking heart would never hurt me intentionally. She would stick to her protocols and do what she thought was right every single time.

It was one of the things I had loved about her, that I still loved about her.

She tucked her phone back into her pocket and looked up.

"So, what's the plan?"

That I did not know.

"Nothing like last time?"

That got a small smile out of her, and I felt some of the heaviness leave my chest. What a fucking bad day.

"No, nothing like last time. If Hayley is really there, we will have to make sure that she doesn't get hurt."

"Agreed," I said, walking back to the bike. "And you can't either."

"Zack, it's my job," she said.

I stopped in my tracks, looking at her. She was right. She was a cop and it was her job to protect and serve.

But she was mine, and I wanted nothing to happen to what was mine. Her eyes widened as I approached her, my hand cupping her cheek roughly before I crashed my lips against hers. I swallowed her gasp, all of my frustration and need channeling into this one kiss. Sydney melted against me as I wrapped my arm around her waist, savoring this one moment between us. All hell was going to break loose soon, but I wanted nothing more than to kiss her.

Her hands landed on my chest, and I forced myself to step back before I fucked her on this bike, out in the open. One day, one day we were going to have sex in a bed. Her eyes were alight with heat, the same heat that was coursing in my veins.

"Zack," she breathed. "What is happening to us?"

"I don't know," I answered hoarsely, tucking her hair behind her ear. "I don't know how to fix this."

I didn't. This was all screwed up, me and her against each other, but it was who we were now as adults.

She nodded.

"Let just... let's get this over with."

I clenched my jaw as I swung my leg over the bike, firing the engine. Sydney pressed against my back, and for a moment I just sat there, savoring the fact that we were just two people caught in two different worlds.

And those two worlds were about to collide.

***

We arrived at the auto shop less than an hour later. I parked the bike off to the side, away from the shop, in case of a quick exit. The auto shop was known to be a staging area for drugs and car theft, the shop just a front for tax purposes, I guessed. Grant owned a piece of the property, which was surprising that the cartel would be using it to hold Hayley. It was ballsy.

"I'll go around back," Sydney said as she checked her gun. "Back up should be here soon."

"Make sure they don't shoot me instead," I grumbled, pulling out my own Glock.

Sydney eyed my gun but said nothing, and I knew what she was thinking. She was thinking about the Muertos that she thought I had killed. I should correct her, but would she believe me?

Sydney straightened her shoulders, rolling her neck before giving me a look.

"Just, don't die; okay, Zack?"

I wanted to tell her to stay here, let me handle it, and that way I wouldn't have that ball of fear growing in my chest at the thought of her in the line of fire. If anything happened to her, I would lose it. There was so much to say to her, so much time to make up.

"If I do, don't put me in one of those damn suits. Bury me in my vest."

"That's not funny," she said in a tiny voice. "I don't... I won't be burying you any time soon."

I winked at her, attempting to ease her concern.

"If you get into trouble, don't wait on me. Get Hayley out of here."

She nodded. "Let's go."

Chapter Seventeen
Sydney

I blew out a breath as I crept behind the auto shop, my gun at my side. I was a bundle of nerves over what we might get into here, what we might find, but also what I was going to do about Zack.

And my feelings.

I wished he had never kissed me. I wished we had never crossed paths. My heart was heavy with what was to come, what I had seen him do, and what he would likely do in the future. There was no way we could be together.

Emotion clouded my vision, and I blinked it away, focusing on the task at hand. If we found Hayley today, then our partnership would be no more. I couldn't pretend that we were the same people any more. We weren't, and it hurt. Oh, it hurt to know that I was going to have to walk away from the only man that had captured my heart.

Clearing my throat, I found a door to the shop, trying the knob. It turned easily under my touch, and I pushed it open, sticking my gun in the open space first before easing inside.

The room was empty, the smell of oil and dank assaulting my senses. I straightened and looked around, seeing nothing but a vast space that hadn't been used in quite a while. Hayley wasn't here.

Stepping back out of the shop, I eyed the warehouse behind it. There were tire tracks in the dirt leading to the building, which wasn't surprising. I knew, along with everyone else in the county, that this area was used for trafficking of all kinds. While we had busted quite a few deals here, we hadn't been able to shut it down completely, so the activity continued.

I walked toward the warehouse, hoping that Zack was watching the front. Ever since the informant had mentioned a possible inside job on Hayley's disappearance, I had been more and more concerned that he might be right. The cartel story… it just didn't make sense.

They already had the upper hand in Cibolo, and if they were wanting to get under Grant's skin, they would have already killed his daughter. The Muertos were not ones to drag something like this out.

It made no sense to include them on this.

I pushed open the door, surprised it wasn't locked, and stepped inside, my gun at my side. My heart seized in my chest as I realized that I was staring at Hayley Travis.

Thank God!

After a quick assessment of the space, I hurried over to her, seeing the relief in her eyes. Pulling down the rag, I started working on her zip ties.

"Thank God," she breathed, her voice hoarse. "That rag was hideously awful!"

"Is there anyone here?" I asked softly, snapping her ties with my knife.

"N-no," she stammered as the door opened.

I turned to see Zack standing there, his gun raised, and surprise written on his face.

"You found her."

It wasn't a question, but more like a resigned statement.

"I did," I swallowed as I snapped the last tie. "Come on, we need to get you out of here."

"Freeze! Police!"

I froze as police started to pour into the warehouse, their guns drawn. I held up my hands, watching as Zack turned to do the same.

"Officer Warren. I've found the missing person."

"Syd?"

Luke stepped forward, lowering his gun.

"Is that you?"

I blew out a breath, giving the young officer a smile.

"It's me. I found Hayley Travis."

"Thank God," Hayley sighed, rubbing her wrists. "It's about time someone found me."

I looked for Zack, but there was a swarm of police filling the building, wondering where he had gotten off to. Likely to report to Grant that his daughter had been found. The chief pushed his way through the crowd, his hefty stomach covered with a bullet proof vest.

"Ms. Travis are you hurt?"

"Of course, I am," Hayley said, wrapping her arms around her tiny waist. "I want to go home."

"We will get you there as soon as we can," the chief promised. "Luke, escort her to the ambulance. Those wounds need to be looked at."

Luke stepped forward and led Hayley away as the chief looked at me.

"Congratulations, Warren. You did it."

I accepted his congrats with a nod.

"There was no one else here. There's still the matter of finding who did this."

The chief nodded.

"I agree. You are going to take the lead on questioning our witness. I need you at the station to clean this mess up and find out who we are after."

"Got it," I said, elation welling up in my chest.

I was happy that Hayley was alive, that she didn't seem to be hurt on the outside. What emotions she would be dealing with would come with time and some good therapy.

"And you will be the one to arrest Hale."

My eyes flew to his face, terror worming its way into my veins.

"W-what?"

The chief looked at me grimly.

"You heard me. He's wanted in an assault earlier today. We have to make a statement, Warren. This cannot be allowed in our town."

I swallowed hard.

"Chief, I was there."

"I know," the chief said heavily, wiping his hand over his face. "But you didn't nearly kill the kid, did you Warren? This is your saving grace to make it up to me. Arrest Hale and show me you can still do this job without getting all emotional. He's a criminal, and he needs to be in jail for what he's done."

"Chief…" I started, unsure of what to say.

Arrest Zack?

He eyed me, sympathy intermixed with regret and anger.

"I told you, Sydney, there might come a time where you have to choose. This is now that time. If you don't arrest him, I will have someone else do it."

"No," I said quickly, holstering my weapon. "I will do it."

It had to be me. I was the only person he wouldn't fight.

The chief handed me a set of cuffs, and I walked through the crowd of police and forensics that had arrived, ready to process the scene. I didn't want to do this, but it had to be done. Zack had stepped out of line by assaulting the kid, and as a result the kid had squealed on him. There was nothing I could do.

Oh, but what I wanted to do was tell him to run, to get away from here. He wouldn't make it far, but now I wished I had told him to back off at the clubhouse and done this myself. At least he would have had a chance to flee.

I found him just outside the warehouse, eyeing a group of cops that were itching to have him step out of line. He saw me and straightened, a grin on his face.

"We found her."

"We did," I said slowly, my heart breaking. "I'm going to have to ask you to turn around, Zack."

His grin slid off his face and his eyes darkened.

"What?"

I held up the cuffs, struggling to get the words out.

"I... you are under arrest for the assault on the informant earlier."

"You're fucking kidding me," he said, his voice low. "You were there. It got us this information."

I shook my head.

"I can't, I have to bring you in Zack."

He took a step closer, and some of the cops moved in, their hands on their guns. I waved them off. That was the last thing I needed right now.

"It's me, Syd."

I swallowed the lump in my throat.

"I know."

His eyes searched mine, and I saw the betrayal in his depths. I hated it.

"You need help, Syd?"

I turned to see Luke standing off to the side, concern on his face. I sucked in a breath and shook my head.

"Turn around Mr. Hale."

Zack swore but did as I said. My hands were shaking as I brought his behind his back and snapped the cuffs on. The sound was loud and grating in my ears, and I wanted to scream in frustration and fury. This wasn't right. This was not what was supposed to happen today.

"You have the right to remain silent," I started instead, seeing the tension on his shoulders.

He was quiet while I went through his rights, my voice sounded odd even to my ears as I rattled off the paragraph by heart.

"Do you have any questions?"

"No," he barked, shifting his stance. "Can we go now?"

Thankfully, Luke came over and grabbed Zack's arm.

"I got him."

I didn't say anything as Luke led Zack away, my heart aching in my chest.

When had this gone wrong?

Chapter Eighteen
Zack

Sydney had arrested me.

I shifted on the hard leather seat, the rage boiling inside.

And my heart… I didn't want to think about the pain in my chest. She had arrested me.

My Sydney.

I let out a groan and leaned my head on the cage in front of me. This was not how the day was supposed to go. I hadn't even told Grant that we had found Hayley unharmed. No, now Sydney would get that chance, and I would have to live with the fact that I had let my mentor down, at least in his eyes.

Shit, this day had gone to shit.

"You know she didn't want to do it."

I raised my head and caught the eye of the police officer in the mirror, the one that was escorting me to jail.

"What the fuck did you say?"

He cleared his throat.

"Sydney, she didn't want to do it. I could see it all over her face."

"And what do you know about her face?"

He let out a chuckle.

"Are you kidding me? I have been her partner since the moment she walked into the station. I tried, but she wasn't interested, so don't even think that's what is going on here."

I exhaled, glad that I wasn't going to have to kill him somehow for messing with Sydney.

"Why do you care?"

He gave a shrug.

"Hell, I don't know. You just look so pissed off about it, and I don't want you to be pissed at her. She struggled with arresting you. I'm sure the chief didn't give her a choice."

I leaned back on the seat. He was probably telling the truth. Though I couldn't see her face, I could hear it in her voice as she read me my rights that she wasn't happy about having to do so.

But she had still done it.

"Don't give up on her," the police officer said quietly. "She's only doing her job."

I didn't want to give up on her. I hadn't planned to do so either. Well, until this. Hell, I was used to going to jail, but to be put there by Sydney? That was a low blow.

The car was silent the rest of the way, the officer not as rough with me as some had been as he escorted me into the station and sat me in one of the interrogation rooms. He hooked the handcuff to the table before walking to the door.

"You need anything?"

"No," I growled, shifting in the chair. "Thanks."

He nodded, pausing at the door on his way out.

"I've got her back, you know. I will watch out for her, until… well, you can get outta here."

I doubted it was going to happen this time.

"Thanks. I appreciate it."

He nodded and shut the door, leaving me alone.

This room didn't have a mirror in it, nothing but four walls that had sound-proof padding lining it. The handcuff clinked against the table leg as I shifted on the hard seat. Hell, would Sydney have to give her testimony to put me behind bars? I didn't want to see that.

And I was sure she wouldn't be a willing partner.

Groaning, I wiped a hand over my face. I was supposed to be telling Grant that we had found Hayley, then figuring out what was left for me and Syd to re-coup in our relationship.

But now… hell, I didn't know what was going to happen. She had always known about my past, something I had shared with her the first few times we had gone out.

Well, when I had thought this was more than just a fuck and run.

***

I nervously drove down the road, wiping one palm on my jeans. Sydney sat next to me, looking fucking gorgeous as always in her short dress, showing me a great deal of her legs in the process. I had requested the dress tonight, wanting to make it special.

After all, you only have one senior prom. I had been drunk off my ass for mine.

"Where are we going?" she asked as I turned down the next road, the truck rumbling over bumps.

"Somewhere," I grinned, looking over at her. "Are you sure you don't want to go back?"

She shook her head.

"If I can't take you to the prom, then I don't want to go."

Inwardly I grinned. Just the thought of her going to that damn dance with anyone else made me clench my jaw. Sydney was mine.

I pulled the truck into the clearing and cut the engine, looking over to see Sydney's face as she saw what I had done.

"Oh my God, Zack. What is this?"

I reached over and brushed her shoulder with my fingers.

"This is your prom, Syd."

She made a sound and threw open the door, stepping out onto the grass. I followed her, my hands in my pockets as she took in the blanket on the ground, the clearing a perfect place to view the stars. I had found an old radio in my dad's house, and it was playing some oldie station, the soft music mingling with the sound of crickets in the grass. Nearby were a couple of plastic cups and a bottle of cheap wine chilling in a bucket of ice. I was glad to see that no one else had disturbed my handiwork.

Sydney turned toward me, and I was surprised to see the tears shining in her eyes.

"You did this for me?"

I nodded, her tears tearing a hole in my chest.

"I did."

She clasped her hands to her chest.

"I can't... no one has ever done anything so nice for me before. This is... wow!"

I closed the gap between us, catching one of her tears with my finger before it reached her chin.

"It's nothing special."

She sniffed, reaching up to cup my cheek.

"It's everything Zack. I-I love you."

Her words cut through me.

"You can't love me."

Her hand tightened on my cheek.

"Why not? You are so good to me and you make me happy."

I stepped out of her reach, pushing a hand through my hair roughly.

"Shit, Syd, I have… I'm not a good guy."

She moved closer, her eyes still shining.

"So, you aren't perfect. Neither am I."

"No," I interrupted her. "It's not that. I'm… hell, I have a record Sydney."

She stopped, and her lips parted.

"A record?"

I hated the look in her eyes. It made feel like an ass for even knowing her.

"I'm a criminal Sydney. I've done things in my life that I'm not proud of."

"Oh," Sydney answered, closing the distance between us. "Is that all?"

I stared at her.

"What?"

Her lips curved in a smile as she slid her arms around my neck, pulling me against her until our bodies were flush together.

"I love you," she said softly. "I don't care if you think you aren't a good guy. I see something in you, Zack, something that keeps me coming back for more."

I was humbled by her words, the earnest look in her eyes.

"Don't ever leave me," I whispered, tightening my hold on her.

"I don't plan to," she laughed, hugging me close.

***

I shook out of the memory, a frown on my face. She hadn't left all those years ago. That night, I had taken the one thing she could give just one person: her virginity. That night, I had whispered words into her ear, promises of the future and what we had in store for us. I had told her how special she was to me, but never once did I tell her that I loved her. No, that had come just two days ago, realizing that I had given up the best damn thing in my life for… what? For this? I had driven her away with my thoughts of grander things with the DHMC. She had left because I had nearly ruined her life, and right now I was ruining her career.

Whether she admitted to it or not.

Why did life have to be so damn complicated?

Tapping my fingers along the steel table, I thought about my current situation. Once word got to Grant, I knew he would try and spring me out of there. But would the charges hold? Was I looking at jail-time? I wasn't scared of jail. Hell, that was where I probably belonged given my record.

But it would put me further away from Sydney and the things she and I needed to discuss. As a police officer, she couldn't have a boyfriend in jail. I would be that black mark on her career, on her life.

We couldn't be together.

"Shit," I muttered to the empty room.

It was true. We couldn't be together. If I went down for this crime, she couldn't be anywhere near me.

The thought didn't settle well with me.

I grabbed two bottles of water from the fridge before shutting the door, my emotions in turmoil. The station was abuzz with activity, all hands on deck in processing the warehouse and the next steps in finding the asshole that had kidnapped Hayley Travis. There were things I had to do, such as interview the victim and get a timeline of events that would aid us in our investigation.

But all I could think about was Zack and the way he had looked at me before I had slapped the cuffs on him and hauled him to jail. My chest literally ached with sadness at this turn of events. Zack had no one other than the club in his life, no one that would come to his aid and bail him out of this one. He couldn't go to prison over the assault, he just couldn't.

Because if he did, I didn't know what I was going to do.

"Hey, Syd."

I turned to see Luke watching me, leaning against the doorway with his arms crossed over his chest.

"Hey. I was just grabbing some waters for our vic."

His eyes grew soft.

"How are you holding up? You okay?"

I swallowed the emotions in my throat, throwing him a small smile.

"Of course. What makes you think I'm not?"

"Oh, I don't know," he mused. "Maybe it has something to do with the fact you had to arrest Zack Hale? Come on Syd, it's plain to see you are in love with him again."

The emotions welled up in my chest, but I tamped them down, not wanting to cry in front of anyone at the moment. The ride over in the patrol car with the chief had been bad enough. I was on overdrive in the emotion department right now, and, I knew that at any moment it was going to be ugly.

I just hoped I could hold it together until I left the station.

"Thanks," I said softly. "For coming to my aid."

"Any time," he said, pushing away from the doorframe. "Hey, he's in room two if you want to see him."

I doubted Zack wanted to see me after what I had done. Giving Luke a nod, I walked out of the breakroom toward the interrogation room where Hayley Travis was sitting. She barely looked at me as I entered the room, and I slid one of the waters across the table, taking a seat in front of her.

"Thought you might be thirsty."

She let out a shuddering breath and took the water, unscrewing the cap.

"Thanks."

I did the same, the cool liquid soothing my parched throat.

"So," Hayley said as she replaced the cap. "You want to know what happened."

"Whatever you wish to tell me," I said evenly, placing my bottle on the table. "Anything that will help catch the person who did this to you."

The petite woman looked at me, and I could see the horror in her eyes, the exhaustion that lined her face. The medical personnel had already informed me that, besides some dehydration and the cuts on her wrists and ankles from the zip ties, she was virtually unharmed. She had also told them that she hadn't been touched sexually, only taunted about it a time or two.

All in all, Hayley Travis had gotten off pretty decent, considering the circumstances.

"I don't know his name," she started out, drawing in a breath. "But he's a Horseman, there's no doubt about it."

I sat up straighter. So, what the informant had told us was true. There was someone on the inside that had turned traitor.

"Did he say why?"

She gave a little shrug.

"Something about wanting to take over my dad's spot. As if that could happen. My dad will kill the asshole as soon as he can find him."

I pulled out my notebook, locating my pen in my shirt pocket.

"Can you give me a description?"

"He was older," she said with a huff, drumming her fingernails on the table. "With gray hair. And he wore one of those half masks, covering up the top half of his face. I don't know, they all look the same when they have gray hair."

I thought back to my visits to the clubhouse. The only ones I had come in contact with that had gray hair were Grant himself and Grayson, the right-hand man. Surely, he wasn't looking to screw over the hand that fed him.

"Would you recognize him again if you had to?" I asked Hayley, scribbling down what she had said.

"Yeah," Hayley responded, her eyes hardening. "I would."

I looked at her. "Did you ever see any members of the cartel around the place? Anyone helping him?"

"I heard voices," she said, a shudder rolling through her body. "I thought they would come in and rape me, you know? But no one ever came in, except him, and never without the mask."

I blew out a breath. It wasn't much of a lead, but it did prove that someone in the DHMC was attempting to thwart the current leadership. What was I going to do with that information? Without a name, it would only cause chaos in their ranks, which could lead to a bloodbath.

Thank God Zack didn't have gray hair.

Just the thought of him tore at my heart. What was he doing in that room? What was he thinking? Did he hate me?

"Hey, cop," Hayley said, catching my attention. "You think I could call my dad?"

"In a minute," I said, handing over my phone to her. "I would rather you call your sister first."

Hayley frowned as she took the cell phone.

"Why?"

"Because," I said, drawing in a breath. "She specifically asked me to work on your case. She should be the first to know that you are okay."

Hayley looked at me with some distrust as she dialed her sister's number. I listened to the conversation, how tearful Amy sounded on the other end as Hayley told her she was okay, wiping away tears herself. That part had a happy ending, though I imagined it had taken some of Hayley's youthfulness away from her. The girl would never forget the time she had spent at the hands of someone that wanted to do her harm and how close she had come to that happening.

Finally, she hung up the call, and I gave her nod to call her father, hoping that he would be just as ecstatic about hearing the news.

"Just don't tell him about who did it," I warned her as she dialed the number.

Hayley looked up.

"Why?"

"Because," I said with a firm tone. "I want to be the one to find the bastard."

Hayley looked at me for a moment and then nodded.

"Okay. I will keep it from him for now, but not for you. For him."

I nodded, and she held the phone up to her ear, breaking out into tears the moment he answered the phone.

While Hayley talked to her dad, my mind drifted back to Zack. If there was a mole inside of the DHMC, I would need his help. As much as I hated to admit it, he was our best chance at figuring out who had taken Hayley and could do it a hell of a lot faster than any of the rest of us.

But that would mean I would have to face him. The last thing I wanted to do was face him in that interrogation room again, placing us on either side of the table and reminding us that there was a chasm between us. Another more devious thought crossed my mind, and I pushed it away. No, I couldn't break him out of here. That would be the end of my career and would likely land both of us in jail.

No, I would have to come up with something else.

Or someone else.

Hayley hung up the phone before pushing it back across the table, wiping her nose on her sleeve.

"Thanks. He's sending someone to get me."

"Good," I nodded, reaching for the phone. "You don't happen to know the number of your father's legal, do you?"

She stared at me.

"Why?"

I bit my lip.

"Because, I think he's needed."

***

Thirty minutes later I was sitting across from Don Monroe.

"So, what you are saying is that I need to plead his case?"

I nodded, crossing my arms over my chest.

"I need his help and I can't have it as long as he is behind bars. You have gotten him off all those other times, get him off the hook now."

Don eyed me.

"You know, this is a very interesting circumstance, a cop asking for my help to spring a Horseman member."

I sighed.

"I know but you can do it, right?"

Don straightened, looking affronted that I had even asked the question.

"Of course, I can. You cops, you never cover all your loopholes. I already looked into it. The informant is going to recant his statement. He fell down the stairs, nothing more."

I let out a laugh.

"Are you serious?"

Don shrugged, a slimy smile on his face.

"Who cares what he says, as long as he says the right things. You want me to go do the paperwork now?"

I shooed him away, and he laughed as he walked through the door, leaving me alone in the room. I had made this call out of desperation, knowing that Don could get Zack freed faster than anyone could. I just hoped Zack didn't want to kill me once he was out, wipe his hands of this case, and move on without a second glance. I didn't care about our relationship presently, but the information I was holding onto… well, I just hoped he would believe me.

Pushing away from the table, I walked out of the room and stood before the other room that Zack was currently in, pressing my eye against the peep-hole to take a glance at him. He was sitting there, looking like he was bored, but I could see the shimmer of anger vibrating off his body.

I had to talk to him.

So why was I hesitating? The last time I brought him in, I had been nearly gloating over the fact.

But this time around, things were different between us.

Oh, why did things have to be so complicated?

"Alright, it's done."

I whirled around to see Don standing in the hall, a grin on his face.

"What? That quickly?"

He nodded.

"What can I say, I'm that damn good."

Ignoring the slimy bastard, I swallowed the lump in my throat as I reached for the knob on the door. I wanted to be the one to tell him that he was free. I wanted to apologize and beg for his help.

Most of all I wanted to hear him say that he forgave me. If he didn't… well, I was going to cry my eyes out in the privacy of my own home.

Maybe it was best. Maybe we weren't going to get back together again.

How could it work anyway, between a cop and a criminal?

Chapter Twenty
Zack

The door opened, and I sat up, expecting the booking officer to walk in and take me to the jail. Instead, it was Sydney walking through the door.

Shit! Surely, they weren't going to do this to me and her both.

"Zack," she said, pulling out a chair.

"Syd," I said slowly, watching her every movement.

She looked nervous, and I swallowed any emotions that were threatening to overflow.

"What are you doing here?"

She sighed, the lines of exhaustion evident on her face. "I got you free."

I was stunned.

"What?"

"I got you free," she repeated, looking at me. "I called Don. He did his magic. They are dropping all charges."

The relief flowed through my veins as I stared at her. Thank God! I was looking at jail-time this time around, my luck having run out.

"I… thank you."

She waved her hand at me.

"There's more. The reason I did it is because I need your help."

"What kind of help?" I asked, scared to find out.

Hell, every time I'd helped her recently I'd ended up here, in cuffs.

She looked at the cuffs and reached for her key, unlocking them from my wrist. The metal clanged against the table, echoing in the small room.

"Thanks."

"You're welcome," she said softly, her eyes mirroring the hurt I was feeling. "I'm sorry Zack. I-I had no choice."

I reached across the table and lightly gripped her hand, rubbing my thumb over the top of her hand.

"Don't worry about it. I'm used to being in cuffs."

She let out a tortured laugh, squeezing my hand. "Please don't say things like that."

"You know it's true," I said softly, in case the room was linked with audio. I wouldn't have been surprised if it was. "I'm an asshole Syd. I've screwed up more times than you probably could count."

She looked at me, the softness in her eyes surprising me.

"I read your file."

Well, of course she did.

"Was it impressive?" I teased.

She flushed.

"It was pretty thick."

I grinned despite my situation, lacing our fingers together.

"And?"

She drew in a breath, looking at our joined hands.

"I don't care. I told you that before. Nothing's changed."

The tightness in my chest loosened just a bit. Sydney wasn't giving up on me. She was the only one in my life that mattered, the only one that I cared what she thought, what she saw when she looked at me.

She cleared her throat, pulling our fingers apart.

"That not my only news."

"How's Hayley?" I interrupted her.

I had only gotten a glimpse of Grant's daughter before she had been whisked away and couldn't tell from my vantage point if the kid had been okay or not.

"She's lucky," Sydney replied. "A few scratches, but nothing that she would need to worry about. That's what I am here for, Zack. She… well, she said that someone on the inside took her."

It took me a minute to understand what she was saying.

"You mean someone in the club?"

She nodded.

"She couldn't see who it was, but he had gray hair and he wants to overthrow Grant and take control of the club. I told her not to tell her dad, but I don't know how long that will last. I, we, need to get to Grant before whoever this is finds out that Hayley is gone."

I swore. Someone in the club was responsible for Hayley's disappearance. I doubted the girl had made that up. Shit. That was not what I needed to hear.

"They probably have already heard."

"You're probably right," Sydney sighed, rubbing her face with her hand. "What a mess."

I couldn't help but agree with her.

"Did she call her father?"

"And Amy," she responded. "I have her still in the room, waiting for someone to come get her. I didn't want to send her out of here without an escort this time."

"Good," I answered, standing. "We need to get over to Grant before this asshole does."

Sydney stood as well, wrapping her arms around her waist.

"I'm sorry Zack. About this. You know I don't want you to be here."

Not caring who saw us, I rounded the table and took her into my arms, forcing her to look at me.

"I know," I said harshly, looking into her eyes. "I know, and I don't like it, but that's who you are, and this is who I am. We will find a way, Syd. Don't give up on us."

"I'm trying not to," she said, her voice crumbling. "What are we going to do?"

I pressed my forehead to hers, breathing in her scent to calm me.

"I don't fucking know, but we will figure it out."

She gripped my forearms tightly before pushing away, walking a good way's away.

"I don't have my jeep, and you don't have the truck, but I can get my hands on a patrol car."

"Good," I said, following her out of the room. "Can I see Hayley."

Sydney looked as if she wanted to deny me that request, but her shoulders sagged, and she pointed to a closed door not far from us.

"She's in there. I will go get the car."

I nodded and turned the knob, pushing it open.

Hayley sat at the table with Don, both of them looking at me as I entered the room.

"So, she did spring you," Don said with a laugh. "One day, they are going to learn."

"She had just cause," I said, looking at Hayley. "Are you okay?"

She nodded.

"I'm fine. Dad told me you were the one on my case. Thank you."

"Don't thank me yet," I replied with a hint of a grin. "I still have to find the bastard."

"And you will," Don cut in.

"Just stay with her," I told the lawyer. "Until you know who is getting her."

I wasn't about to tell him what I knew, but I did know that he would protect her with his life. We all would, no matter how annoying she got.

"Thank you, Zack," Hayley said again as I walked out of the room.

I found Sydney in the hall. She dangled the keys in front of her and I took them.

"You are going to let me drive?"

She smirked.

"Don't get used to it. I don't know where I am going."

I gave her a wink as we walked to the front desk, where I got my things in a clear plastic bag. Reaching in, I pulled out my cell phone and Glock, tucking it in my waistband as we walked outside. Almost immediately, my phone vibrated in my hand.

"Yeah," I said, holding it up to my ear.

"Cartel is on the move," Grayson said into my ear. "I think they are heading to the Travis house. Word is out that Hayley has been rescued."

"Shit," I swore as Grayson hung up.

"What?" Sydney asked as she led me to the car.

"That was Grayson," I answered her, opening the door on the borrowed car. "Cartel is on the move."

Sydney climbed in to the passenger seat, and I cranked up the car.

"What if he's lying?"

I looked over at her, raising an eyebrow.

"You think he's the kidnapper?"

"Gray hair, right-hand man, it all fits," she answered as she buckled up. "Think about it. Who sent us to the informant? Who is sending us on this mission? What if it's Grayson that wants the club?"

I didn't answer her as I pulled out of the parking spot, pointing the car toward the Travis home. She did have a point. But Grayson? He knew everything about the club, about the brotherhood and his president. Grant included him in everything he did. Surely, he hadn't faked a turf war just to get the cartel and DHMC fighting so that he could rise to the top. That would take some balls and a shit-load of planning.

"You are thinking about it," Sydney said quietly as I turned down the street.

"It doesn't make sense," I muttered.

"The whole thing hasn't made any sense," Sydney added, reaching for her phone. "I'm going to call for backup."

"Tell them not to arrest me this time," I growled reaching for my own phone and dialing the clubhouse.

There was no answer, only a recording that the line was busy and could not be reached.

"I can't reach the house."

"Backup is on its way," Sydney replied, throwing her phone on the dash. "What if it's Grayson? What will you do?"

I gripped the steering wheel, dodging a car in front of me.

"Then I will kill the son of a bitch."

Inside I hoped it was not him. Grant would be heartbroken, and the club would begin to worry if anyone could be trusted. A traitor in the midst usually meant more than one traitor was there.

Turning down the next street, I slammed on the brakes as I saw the blockade in the middle of the road.

"Get down!" I shouted at Sydney, reaching for my gun.

Sydney ducked as a spray of bullets hit the car. I threw the car in reverse, firing a few rounds out the window before pushing the car away from the danger. The car careened wildly before I crashed it into a fence, the airbags deploying a second later.

Sydney coughed and fought her bag as I opened the door, using it as a shield as the gunfire got closer. Shit. We were trapped. We could run, but I didn't know how far we would get before they hunted us down.

I had to get Sydney out of here.

"Zack!" she shouted from the other side of the car, the bullets pinging the front of the car. "We have to get out of here!"

"I'm thinking!" I shouted back, firing a few rounds in the direction of the gunfire. There were a few houses on this road, some that would provide ample coverage while we waited for someone to show up.

"You see those houses to your right?"

"Yes!" she shouted back, firing off a few rounds. "Are we going for cover?"

"Unless you have a better plan! On the count of three!"

I fired a few more rounds before looking over at Sydney.

"One, Two, Three!"

She took off as I rounded the back of the car, firing over the top and striking one of the cartel members that were firing back. He fell back with a yelp, and I took off, the spray of bullets following closely behind.

Hell, if we didn't get any help soon we would be sitting ducks.

I reached the corner of the first house, catching up with a wide-eyed Sydney, who had her back pressed against the cool stone.

"You okay?"

"I'm fine," she said with a grim smile. "You?"

"No holes," I joked, checking my bullet count.

I had no back-up ammo on me and I doubted Sydney had any either.

That, and she wasn't wearing a vest today.

"Tell me you have a plan."

"N-no," Sydney replied. "I don't have a plan other than hope that they run out of bullets first. Where is the backup?"

That I was wondering myself. A bullet pinged off the brick beside my head, and I peeped around the corner, killing another gringo that had gotten too close. We weren't going to die here today.

Looking over at Sydney, I drank her in before reaching for her.

"You go on, run. I will hold them off."

She looked at me, horrified.

"What? No. We don't leave each other this time. We are both in this together."

"Syd," I swallowed. "You have to go."

"No," she said firmly, shrugging off my touch. "It's either the both of us or nothing at all, Zack."

I stared at her as she returned some fire, her gun flashing to rapid succession of shots. What had I done in my miserable life right to deserve someone like her?

Turning my attention back to the threat, I counted the bullets in my head, carefully firing off rounds that would hit their mark. Once the bullets ran out, I would force Sydney to run. I couldn't allow her to die out here today.

Me, I would go willingly, as long as I knew she was safe.

A dull roar filled the air and I laughed as the multitude of bikes tore down the road, all scrambling for cover as the groups of cartels resumed their fire.

"It's the backup."

"The club," Sydney breathed, lowering her gun. "They are here."

Chapter Twenty-One
Sydney

We weren't going to die after all.

I checked the bullets in my gun once more, noting the very few I had left. Below us, the sound of gunfire filled the air as the turf war raged on. I watched in amazement as the bikers hid expertly in the spaces they could find as the cartel fired on them, much like the maneuvers we used in the police academy. The club seemed not as prepared for what they were walking into and I bit my lip.

They were going to get slaughtered.

"I have to go help," Zack said suddenly, looking at me. "Cover me."

"Zack, no," I begged, grabbing his arm. "You will get killed."

"I have to try," he said, touching my cheek. "I love you. Dammit Syd, I do."

My breath stuttered in my chest. He couldn't say something like that and then go charging down there into the fray.

"Please don't go."

He gave me a dead stare, so many emotions crossing his face.

"Stay here."

"Zack!" I yelled as he took off toward his brotherhood. I fired a few rounds toward the melee, sobs tearing at my throat as I watched him. I could not lose him now.

Not when I had finally found him.

Suddenly, he went down, and I nearly lost it, tearing out of my hiding place toward him, my heart in my throat. No. I couldn't lose him. This could not be happening.

Sirens blazed in the distance, and I knew it was my own backup coming, but I didn't care. Dodging the bullets, I reached his side, a sob escaping me as I saw the spread of blood on his chest. Oh God, he had been shot!

"Zack!" I yelled, shaking him. "Dear God, open your eyes!"

His eyes fluttered, but I could see the pain reflecting in them, the rapidly growing paleness of his face. This was bad.

"Is he hit?"

I looked up to see a biker I didn't recognize at my side, ducking as a bullet whizzed by.

"Help me."

He nodded and grabbed Zack by the arm, slinging him over his shoulder.

"Let's go."

We tore across the grassy field toward a truck, moving farther away from the gunfire. My blood was pumping throughout my body as the biker laid Zack in the back of the truck, jumping in.

"Drive."

I took one look at Zack's pale face, the blood coating his body and jumped in the driver seat, grateful to find the keys in the ignition. Likely they had fled at the sound of the gunfire.

Turning over the engine, I tore down the road, past the gunfight and to the highway, tears streaking my face. I couldn't lose him now.

It wasn't fair. There was so much I had to tell him, so much that we owed each other.

***

Hours later, I sat in the intensive care room with Zack, holding his cold hand in my own. He was hooked up to all kinds of tubes and lines, a breathing machine keeping him breathing while the heart monitor beeped out a rhythm. Zack looked nothing like the tough biker I knew him to be, his entire chest wrapped in white bandages, his skin waxy pale. I had cried enough in the last four hours to fill a damn lake, and even now I felt the tears leak from my eyes, dripping down my cheeks and onto the borrowed scrubs that had been given to me. My clothing was in a bag on the floor, soaked with Zack's blood.

I still couldn't believe what was happening.

Rubbing a thumb over the top of his hand, I watched as his chest rose and fell with the breathing machine, wondering if he would ever be the same. The doctors had said he was lucky, that the bullet had nicked an artery, but not tearing through it completely. If it had, he would have never made it to the hospital. The bullet had lodged in his chest right above his tattoo, and it had taken two hours just to remove the damn thing and stop the bleeding. They said Zack had lost over half his blood volume, and I believed it.

The scene had been ugly, and every time I closed my eyes I saw him falling in that field, the blood all over him. I had nearly lost him.

"Oh Zack," I breathed, wishing he would open his eyes to let me know he was still in there.

He was heavily sedated to allow for the healing to begin, but I just wanted to know that everything was going to be alright in the end.

That I wasn't going to lose him.

"Shit."

I turned to see Grant Travis walk into the room, his face pale as he looked at Zack. The president of the Horsemen looked haggard, much older than I remembered, and nothing like the confident man I knew him to be.

"Is he?"

"He's not out of the woods yet," I said softly as he approached the bed. "Another day or so and they will know the damage."

He fell into the chair beside the bed, wiping his hand over his face. I was surprised to see the glimmer of tears in his eyes.

"When they said he had gotten shot, I couldn't believe it. The kid was bullet-proof."

"No one is bullet-proof," I replied, pressing a kiss to Zack's hand, hoping that he could feel that I was here. "H-he tried to save lives."

"We lost many today," Grant said after a moment, emotion in his voice. "Five in all."

"I'm sorry," I said seeing the grief on his face. "I know it's hard."

He turned toward me.

"You love him, don't you?"

I nodded, my heart constricting.

"I do, very much so."

I really was starting to believe I had never stopped loving him.

Grant stared at me for a moment.

"Good, he deserves to be happy. Can I tell you something, Sydney? He's never truly been happy at the club. I would never kick him out. He's like a son to me. But from the moment he walked in that door, I knew something was missing, and I believe that something was you."

I swallowed the tears that clogged my throat.

"He wanted nothing more than to be a Horseman."

Grant laughed softly, leaning back in the chair.

"He will always be a Horseman. He will always have the brotherhood at his back, but he almost didn't have you in his heart."

I watched as the older man looked at the man in the bed fondly, as if he did truly care.

"Do you know that I went with him that night he got the tattoo of your initials?"

Now that surprised me.

"Why?"

He shrugged.

"I don't know. It was my idea actually. I knew I had screwed you over by our little initiation and knew he had lost something very important to him. What better way than to remember you by?"

"I-I lost everything," I forced out, feeling as if he needed to know. "I was prepared to do whatever he wanted after graduation, but after the word got out I couldn't face him or this town."

"I'm sorry," Grant sighed. "I don't know what else to say."

I ran my hand over Zack's again, thinking about the bitterness I had carried around for years for this town, the man in the bed, and the man in the chair. I had hated them all for what they had done to me, but now... well, it didn't matter. I wasn't walking away any more. I needed Zack. I needed to stay in this town.

Grant stood and walked over to the bed, lightly touching Zack's shoulder, careful to avoid the bandages.

"Get better," he said softly. "So, you can give me hell about what I couldn't see right in front of me."

"It was an insider," I said as Grant stepped back. "You know who."

Grant looked at me, his mouth set in a firm line.

"I do. It was Grayson. He kidnapped my daughter, he did this shit to Zack, he got my men, his brothers, killed today. I will not rest until his head is on my desk."

I shivered at the coldness in his eyes. I wasn't about to tell him what he wanted to do was wrong. After what happened today, I would happily help him hunt down the bastard.

Grant walked toward the door, stopping to look back at me.

"Let me know when he wakes, will you?"

"I will," I said softly.

He gave me a nod and disappeared through the doorway, leaving me to watch over Zack once more. Grant might be a hard ass, but it was clear to me that he did care about the man in the bed.

Though no one could love him as much as I did.

I just wanted the opportunity to tell him so.

***

The next day, the chief stopped by.

"How are you holding up?" he asked as he stepped inside the room.

I sighed, looking over at the bed.

"I'm okay. He's doing better and survived the night."

"Good," Chief Turner said, hooking his thumbs into his belt loops. "He's a lucky bastard."

My eyes drifted over Zack's body, from the top of his head to the sheet that covered his legs.

"He is chief."

He cleared his throat, looking over at me.

"You know that they coerced that kid into recanting his statement. I was forced to drop all charges against Zack Hale."

Inwardly I sighed in relief.

"What about me?"

He arched a brow.

"What about you? You didn't do anything wrong. He was a free man at that point."

"But I was the one that called Don Monroe," I blurted out. "I got the charges dropped."

"Sydney," the chief started, shaking his head. "We all know why you did it, and honestly I can't say that I blame you. You two are meant to be together, and no matter what kind of advice I give you, you are going to ignore it in favor of what's in your heart."

I swallowed hard. My heart felt like it had been ripped out of my chest. Until Zack opened his eyes, I would be hurting something fierce, scared that I was going to lose him.

"What about my job?"

"What about it?"

"Surely, I can't... I mean, I can't be with him and be a cop as well," I stammered.

I would choose Zack all day long if need be, but not being a cop...? It hurt.

"Well, about that," Chief Turner said with a wry smile. "I think we can work out something. Maybe I will drum up a new task force that works closely with our biker friends. I think you would be a good fit for that one."

I could have hugged him.

"Are you sure?"

"You are a good cop," he stated, walking to the door. "But I'm not one to tell you to choose between your heart and your career. We will work it out, Sydney. You concentrate on getting this man here well enough to help out."

Tears sprang to my eyes.

"Thank you chief."

"See you in a few weeks," he said. "You are officially on family leave, and I expect you to take full advantage of it."

I watched him leave, some of the tension easing in my shoulders. I wasn't going to have to choose. I wasn't losing my job.

Life was almost okay.

I walked over to the bed, laying my hand on his forehead and smoothing back his hair. The doctors this morning had stated that in another day or so they would wake him up. I couldn't wait. I couldn't wait to see his eyes on me, to know that he was going to be the same Zack I knew, plus one bullet hole now. Pain racked my body as I touched his face, careful not to disturb any of the lines running in and out of him.

"You have to get better," I whispered. "You have to come back to me."

If he didn't, I didn't know what I would do.

Chapter Twenty-Two
Zack

I snapped my eyes open, wincing as the shaft of sunlight pierced my sluggish brain. My body felt like it had been run over by a truck and there was a searing pain across my chest, one that ached even without moving.

Turning my head, I felt myself start to breathe as I saw Sydney curled up in the chair next to me, her hand touching mine. She looked exhausted, the rings of dark purple evident under her closed eyes.

But she was alive and looked virtually unharmed.

Me, on the other hand…

I looked down the length of my own body, noting the new bandages that covered my chest, feeing the pinpricks of pain now that I was awake. I was in a hospital bed and, by the looks of it, had been here for a while. My mouth felt like sandpaper, and the nauseating stench of medication hung heavily in the air. I fought the urge to move an inch, not wanting to wake Sydney just yet. What the hell had happened? The last thing I remembered was running to meet my brotherhood and join in the fight, before what seemed like a truck had come out of nowhere and slammed into my chest.

Apparently, I had been shot.

Shit. I looked up at the ceiling, adjusting to the pain that was courting the fringes of the medication that was moving through my body. What happened after I'd gone down? It had to have scared Syd shitless. What about her job? Was she screwed because she'd helped me? I didn't know how long I had been out, but just the pure sight of her next to me told me she hadn't given up on us, on me.

Even after all the hell I had put her through.

I thought about the night I had told her I was going to join the Horsemen, the last night before all hell had broken loose and driven the wedge between us. She had been disappointed, begged me not to do it, and I had ignored her.

If only I hadn't ignored her, we wouldn't have been in the position we were in that day.

***

"Say something."

Sydney removed her hand from mine and slid down off the tailgate, wrapping her arms around her body.

"I-I don't know what to say."

I ground my teeth. I wasn't surprised by her reaction. Sydney had to think through all of her decisions, and mine had hit her out of the blue.

But I hoped she would at least understand.

"I know it's not college, but it's a family and they will take care of us, Syd, for life."

She looked up and I saw a glimmer of tears in her eyes.

"But at what cost Zack? For you to do their dirty work? Even kill people? Can you live with that, because I can't? I can't live with the thought of you being in constant danger."

I pushed off the tailgate and placed my hands on her upper arms, finding her trembling.

Shit!

"Nothing is going to happen to me, I swear it. And you can stay here, in Cibolo, and get that degree you want. We can be together, Syd."

Her eyes met mine, and she let out a breath.

"What if I beg you not to do this, Zack?"

I swallowed. Not be a Horseman? Get some shit job so that I could provide a decent life for me and Sydney and whatever came in the future? I wasn't cut out for the decent life, which was what had driven me to look into joining the notorious biker gang. My initial meetings (mostly run-ins in the bars, lending a hand when they needed additional muscle) had gone well. Even last night I had helped them drive out some rogue bikers from the bar near the highway. My knuckles were still busted up from the numerous times I had hit that one guy.

If Sydney had noticed them, she hadn't said anything.

"This is what I should do with my life," I said slowly.

Her eyes held mine just a bit longer, and the disappointment in hers nearly tore me in two.

"What the hell do you want me to do, Syd?" I said softly. "I'm not this guy who holds down a normal job. I have a shit record, barely a high school degree, and no money in the bank. How am I supposed to support you with that?"

She stepped out of my reach, rubbing her hands over where I had been touching her.

"I-I don't want you do this."

I clenched my jaw.

"I'm gonna do it, Syd. It's my only option."

She swallowed, and I wasted no time closing the distance between us, pulling her into my arms. I knew she was upset, but I was going to kiss it out of her. I was going to show her that I could have her and the brotherhood at the same time.

I needed her to not give up on me. Or us, for that matter.

I blinked out of the memory, shifting my arms to get a better position. Sydney's hand jerked on mine, and I turned my head to see her staring at me.

"You're awake."

I grinned. God, even that hurt.

"I guess I am."

She exploded out of the chair, touching my face.

"Are you okay? Are you in pain? Do you need me to get the doctor?"

I reached up to touch her chin, wincing as the pain followed the movement.

"Yes… no… no, not yet. What the hell happened?"

Her eyes clouded with pain, and she swallowed.

"You were shot in the chest. The bullet, it nicked an artery and you nearly bled out before I could get you here."

Well, shit! I had almost died. Swallowing that piece of information, I looked at her.

"What about the brotherhood?"

"A few dead," she answered softly, her expression sympathetic. "It was Grayson. He was the one that kidnapped Hayley and nearly killed you."

The pain in my chest didn't even compare to the pain in my heart. The man who had been my mentor, Grant's right hand man had been responsible.

"Did they… is he dead?"

She shook her head.

"No, but everyone is searching for him and tracking down those that were in cahoots with him. It's going to be a process."

I blew out a breath. I would join that search as soon as I got out of the hospital. I wanted to see Grayson go down for what pain he had caused all of us, all while he pretended that he was on our side. He would suffer for what he had done.

I gazed at Sydney.

"What about you?"

She gave a little shrug.

"I'm fine, now that you are awake and know who you are. It's been a rough week. I'm not going to lie."

A fucking week. No wonder she looked like hell.

"I'm sorry."

She laughed.

"Don't be. I'm just glad you are back with us. You scared the shit out of me that day, Zack. I-I thought I had lost you."

My heart twisted as I saw her pain, hating that I had put her through that. She had begged me not to go, and I had done it anyway, much like the majority of our time together. When was I going to listen to her? She had been right, time after time.

God, I didn't deserve her. I had nearly ruined her life, her career, and caused her nothing but pain and heartache.

She deserved better. I held onto the hope that she could make me feel better about what I was doing, but drug her through the mud right along with me.

"They say you can get out in a few days," she responded as I dropped my touch from her skin, mourning the loss of contact. "I can take you to my house."

I clenched my teeth, my heart screaming 'No!' to what I was about to do. It was the right thing, even if it was going to hurt like hell to do so.

"No need. I'll call the club."

She looked taken aback.

"But I can take care of you there."

I gave her a dead-on stare, wincing inwardly as I saw the pain and confusion in her eyes. She needed to hate me. It was the only way she was going to move on with her life.

"I'm good. I appreciate you keeping this vigil. But now that I'm not dead, I think we should call this a clean break."

Her gaze narrowed.

"What are you talking about?"

"This thing," I forced out, nearly choking on the words. "It's not working for either of us."

"B-but you told me you loved me," she shot back.

I braced my hands on the bed and pushed upward, pain shooting in my chest.

"I do love you, but I can't be with you. You know that, and I know that."

Tears gathered in her eyes, and I felt each one of them inside my soul, fucking hating myself for what I was doing to her. This way, she could be free to find that life she had always dreamed about, the life I couldn't give her.

Even if I was going to suffer in the process.

"I can't believe this," she said, gathering up her things and shoving them in her bag. "After all I have done. I should have known better."

"We knew it wasn't going to last," I said softly, my heart breaking with every damn word.

Sydney looked up, tears streaking down her face.

"Maybe *you* thought that, but I thought that this was forever."

Hell, I wanted it to be. I wanted nothing more than to marry her.

"Things change."

She stared at me a moment longer before walking out of the room. I released a breath and beat my head against the pillow, hating myself for what I had just done to her. Again.

But I was toxic to her life. There was no part of me that was good enough to be with Sydney. I couldn't let her be a victim one day of some drug raid or watch me get arrested for some dumb shit because of the brotherhood. Not only that, there would be a time, much like this time, that our two careers would intertwine and one of us would wind up getting hurt.

It was better like this. This was what I deserved.

Even if it felt like I had just watched my soul walk out of that hospital room.

***

Two weeks later, I walked out of the hospital under my own power. A car was waiting for me and I climbed in, feeling a bit short-winded from the walk. I hadn't realized what laying in bed for two weeks would do to your body.

That, and I couldn't sleep for shit.

"Well, you did it."

I looked over at Grant.

"They haven't killed me yet."

"Good to know," Grant chuckled as the car pulled away from the curb. "Heard you can't ride your bike for a month."

I frowned. The doctor had told me that before he discharged me, stating that the strain of reaching for the handles could undo all the pieces he had painstakingly put back together. Actually, I wasn't allowed to drive at all, which was damn near killing me.

"What the doc doesn't know won't kill him."

"But it might kill you," Grant said dryly as I leaned back on the leather seat. "What the hell are you doing, Zack?"

Surprise, I looked over at him.

"What do you mean?"

"You're an asshole," he stated, shaking his head. "That woman, she sat by your stubborn ass for a week, taking care of you, and you let her walk out of your room like that? What are you thinking?"

Sydney. I drew in a breath to ease the ache in my chest. It had been two weeks since she had walked out of my hospital room with a broken heart, two weeks since I had felt like anyone gave a damn about me while I recovered. Sure, the brotherhood had stopped by occasionally, giving me hell for getting shot, but there was no one who truly cared about me.

"It's better this way."

"For who?" Grant asked softly. "You look like shit, and I hear she's packing her stuff to leave town again."

"She's leaving?" I asked, surprised.

"Yeah," Grant said coldly, his eyes hardening as he looked at me. "I've done some shitty things in my life, you know. I've lied, cheated, even killed for this brotherhood, but I have never broken a woman's heart because of it. My Lydia is part of this world, and she understands the consequences of being involved with me. But you want to know something? I would give up this shit in a heartbeat if she asked me to. I would walk away because, without her, I'm nobody. I've cheated on her in my younger days, but she stayed by my side, patched up my body, and told me that I better come back home to her every night. For twenty years, I have done that."

I was surprised at his declaration. Grant Travis was the Horsemen. Without him at the helm, the brotherhood didn't exist.

And he was willing to give it all up for a woman.

"Think about it," Grant finished, leaning against the seat. "Why do you get up in the morning, Zack? Why do you have those damn initials tattooed on your skin? Why are you walking out of this hospital today and not six feet under?"

Shit. He was right. Everything I did, especially now, was because of and for Sydney. She had put her career on the line for me, and now I had her running again.

Because of me.

"I'm a fucking asshole," I groaned, wiping a hand over my face.

"That's not the words I would use," Grant chuckled as the car made a turn. "You get one chance in life to find something that keeps you human in this shitty world. Lydia is the only reason I'm the man I am today. I only wish I had half her strength and love that she gives me and our daughters on a daily basis."

I looked at the head of the brotherhood I had wanted to be part of, the life that had pushed me through all these years.

"I need a favor."

He laughed, rolling down the window.

"Already taken care of."

I looked out the window at the house that Sydney was renting, a slow grin spreading across my face.

"You knew I would ask."

"I knew I was going to beat the shit out of you if you didn't," he replied, his eyes full of laughter. "Go on, go get her, and this time don't let her go or you will have to answer to me."

A criminal protecting a cop. That's not something you heard every day.

"Thanks."

He nodded as I climbed out of the car, grabbing my bag before stopping on the sidewalk. What was I going to say? How was I going to grovel to her so that she would take me back this last time? I had ruined her life more times that I cared to count, broken her heart when she needed me the most, and she had every right to slam the door in my face.

But this time, I wasn't going away. I would sit on her damn doorstep if I had to until she took me back, but I wasn't going to let this opportunity slip through my fingers. I loved her, and I was an asshole for doing what I did two weeks ago.

Now I would have to prove to her that she needed me just as much as I needed her.

Chapter Twenty-Three
Sydney

I laid the plate on the counter and wrapped it in the newspaper before placing it in the box, forcing myself to move on to the next one. I hated packing, wanting to throw everything out the back door and walk away, start over.

But my checking account didn't allow for that, and until I found another position somewhere else, I was going to have be careful about spending my money.

The chief had raised hell when I turned in my resignation, telling me not to give up on this job and to forget that Zack Hale had ever existed.

I wished I could. My life would be so much better.

And now, I was heading back to my parents' house, to stay with them until I could get back on my feet. They had accepted me without even asking a question, but I knew they would be asking once I was back under their roof. What was I going to say? That Zack Hale had broken my heart once again, and I hadn't learned my lesson about trusting him?

It sounded weak and pathetic coming out of my mouth like that. I had thought that this time around things would be different, that when he had said he loved me it was going to be forever this time. I loved him with every shuddered breath I breathed, but it didn't change the fact that he didn't want to be with me.

That he didn't truly love me in the first place.

Swallowing the tears that threatened, I placed the next plate on the newspaper and wrapped it carefully, depositing it in the box. It didn't matter anymore. I was going to move away from Cibolo permanently and attempt to forget that these past few months had ever happened. I should have never come back, thinking that I could change this town and those that lived in it.

It was clear to me that my past was always going to come back to haunt me.

A knock on the door sounded throughout the silent house, and I sighed. If it was Luke again, I was just going to shoot him and get over with it. He had come by every day since I had turned in my resignation, attempting to talk me into staying with the force and staying in Cibolo. He didn't understand.

No one did.

Stalking to the door, I threw it open.

"I already told you I'm not staying."

But instead of Luke, Zack was standing there, leaning against the doorjamb.

"Hey, Syd."

My heart stopped in my chest as I eyed him, seeing the effects of his hospital stay on his handsome face. He looked exhausted, his eyes wary as he stared at me.

But there was some color in his face, and he was upright, which was far better than the last time I had seen him.

"What do you want?" I asked flatly, itching to slam the door in his face.

"I don't deserve any of your time," he said with a sigh. "But can I have five minutes?"

I crossed my arms over my chest.

"Why should I give you anything?"

He had broken my heart, pretty much told me he wanted nothing to do with us, and now he wanted to talk?

"Hell, I don't know," he answered honestly, a raw emotion in his eyes. "All I can do is ask."

I knew I should make him leave. I was too unstable, my emotions like a rollercoaster in my heart and soul. He was tearing me in two.

But after today, after this moment, I wouldn't see him again. Whatever he wanted to say would be the last words we would have between us, and I wasn't the Sydney with stars in her eyes any longer.

"Fine," I said, stepping aside. "Five minutes."

He stepped inside, and I shut the door, my house suddenly feeling smaller with him in it.

"I would offer you a seat," I said, sweeping my hand across the room. "But, as you can see, I have nowhere to sit."

"It's fine," Zack said, clearing his throat. "What I have to say won't take long."

His gruff tone was like a dagger to my heart, and idly I wondered if he was going to blast me again like he had in the hospital room. After everything I had done for him during that week, begging God to not take him from me, he had pretty much told me that he no longer wanted this relationship. Oh, it had hurt something bad. To be told that all the hard work you had put into something had been for naught, it burned me deep down inside. I had thought… well, I had been wrong.

So, why was I allowing him to be in my house right now?

He shoved a hand through his hair, looking into my eyes.

"I don't know where to begin, so I am just going to say it and the hell with everything else. I am sorry. I'm an asshole for saying those things to you that day in the hospital. I don't want this to end. I don't want you to leave Cibolo. I want you to stay, deal with my hard ass, and maybe one day marry me. I love you, Sydney, and I will never, ever love anyone the way that I love you."

His words were raw and harsh, but I could feel his frustration come out with every word. A glimmer of hope flared in my chest, but I wasn't about to let him get off that easy.

"You hurt me."

"God, I know," he said, anguish in his eyes. "I'm not good for you. I nearly cost you your job and… hell, Syd, I'm far from the man that you should be with."

"That's for me to decide," I said angrily. "Not you. I gave you everything, Zack. I'm tired of having it thrown back in my face."

"I know," he repeated, pleading with eyes. "Give me one more chance. I swear to you, I will never walk away again. If you want me to leave the club, I will."

"Truly?" I asked with some hesitation.

We had gone down this road before and he had told me no.

He reached out, his fingers touching my cheek.

"Yes," he said firmly. "I will give it all up to be with you."

A sob tore at my throat and I launched myself at him, careful to avoid his injuries.

"Why did you push me away?"

Zack's arms came around me and locked me against him.

"Because I'm stupid and thought I was protecting you, giving you what you deserved."

I wanted nothing more than to be with him. His hand brushed over my hair as I breathed in his scent, some of the tension seeping out of my bones.

"I will kill you if you ever do that to me again."

He chuckled.

"I want you to."

Pulling back, I looked at Zack.

"I quit my job."

He smiled tenderly.

"I know. You are going to have to beg for forgiveness."

"I should send you in there to do it for me."

"I will," Zack answered, brushing his lips over mine. "I will do anything you ask."

I savored his kiss, my heart full for the first time in a long, long while.

"Didn't you mention something about having sex in a bed next time?"

His eyes grew warm.

"You will have to be careful."

I smiled and tugged on his arm, leading him to the bedroom.

"I won't cause you too much pain."

"God, I love you," he said as I pulled my t-shirt over my head.

His throat bobbed as I stripped off my clothes, until I was standing naked before him. There was no shame, no regret.

There was only love.

Walking toward him, I helped Zack get his clothes off, careful not to disturb the small bandage that was above his tattoo.

"I thought I lost you," I whispered, emotion clogging my throat.

He laid a hand over mine, squeezing it lightly.

"I'm not going anywhere."

I believed him this time.

Finally, he was naked before me, my fingers grazing over his powerful shoulders.

"You're beautiful."

Zack leaned down and kissed me softly.

"Not as beautiful as you. I want to worship your body, Syd."

Shyly, I ran a hand down the length of his body, until I had him in my grasp. Zack let out a strangled sound as I explored his hardness, rubbing my thumb over his bulging head.

"It's been a while."

He chuckled, his hand roaming down my body possessively, like an old friend.

"Not that long."

With a little push he steered me to the bed, forcing me to lie down on the mattress. I watched with bated breath as he dropped to one knee before me, spreading my legs with his hands.

"It's time to make you scream, Syd," he whispered, pressing a kiss on the inside of my knee.

I grabbed a fistful of the comforter as his lips travelled up my thigh until they brushed my molten core, whimpering as his tongue delved into the slit.

"Zack."

His hand roamed up my body and grabbed my breast, his tongue lightly circling my clit. I could feel the pressure building and grasped his hair in my fingers to pull him away. He held firm, his hand clamped down on my hip and pulling me toward his mouth, covering the area with his lips. I closed my eyes and let go, screaming his name as the orgasm hit me, his tongue stoking the waves that rippled through my body.

Oh, dear God!

When he covered my body with his, I was barely pushing through the fog of the orgasm.

"Should you be doing this?" I whispered as he towered over me, his cock pressing into my entrance.

"I don't fucking care," he said, pushing the rest of the way. I arched against him, my hands clamoring to grab his shoulders as he filled me to the hilt, forcing another orgasm before I could breathe.

For a moment, we stared at each other, my eyes wet with unshed tears at what was happening.

"I love you," he said through clenched teeth. "Today, tomorrow, always. You are mine, Sydney."

I pulled him down toward me, brushing my lips over his and tasting my own self on his lips.

"Always."

He growled and started to move, the bed jerking with the movement as I clung to him, taking all he had to give. I wasn't worried about what our future might hold, or that one day I might lose him.

I was only focused in this one moment, wrapped in his love.

When he came, I felt the waves crash over me too.

"God," he said after a moment, carefully rolling onto his side.

I snuggled against him, sex heavy in the air.

"I'm going to pay for that."

I giggled.

"I told you so."

His hand brushed lazily over my stomach, drawing little circles around my belly button.

"I don't fucking care. I wasn't waiting another minute."

I turned to face him, cupping his cheek with my hand.

"Are you sure about this?"

He grinned.

"Having second thoughts now that you had a piece of me?"

I slapped him on his shoulder.

"No, I just… what if life tears us apart?"

He leaned over and kissed me.

"Then we will figure it out together, Syd. I'm tired of losing you."

Tears sprang to my eyes.

"I love you so much."

His expression grew tender, and I saw the love reflected in his eyes. My big, bad biker loved me. There was no doubt about it.

"Marry me."

"W-what?"

He captured my hand, kissing it.

"I don't have a fucking ring, nor do I have a crystal ball to tell you that our future is going to be perfect by any means. But I do know I love you, and that's all I can offer you. Marry me, Syd. Don't ever let me feel how it feels to not have you by my side."

A tear slipped down my cheek, and I nodded, rewarded with another kiss.

"I… yes. I will marry you, Zack."

I wanted to give him everything he should have had in his life. A life full of love and happiness, a family that loved him no matter what he did, and the support he needed to keep going. I wanted to be with him when we had our first child, to see the wonderment in his eyes as he held his son or daughter in his arms. I wanted to be there when they went off to college or got married and be the person that held his hand after our house was empty.

Most of all, I wanted to leave this life knowing I had loved him truly and fully, holding his hand right up to the end.

We might not have the same goals and aspirations, but we had love, and love was enough.

Chapter Twenty-Four
Zack

One Year Later

"God, you are lazy as fuck. When are you going to get out of this bed?"

I grinned as I gave Sydney a pat on her ass, sitting next to her on the bed. She gave me the eye, the one that meant she could skewer me alive before rolling over.

"I worked all night. Give me a break."

I rubbed her back lightly.

"It's after three o'clock, and I have waited all day to spend some time with you. Give me a break."

She threw a pillow at me, and I caught it, laughing. If I had learned anything over the past year, I had learned that Sydney was a horrible person when I woke her up after a shift.

Well, unless I was fucking her. That was when she was most agreeable to anything I was doing.

She sighed and rubbed a hand over her face, staring up at me.

"What do you want to do today?"

I gave a little shrug, leaning down to kiss her.

"Maybe we can go for a ride, get something to eat. How does that sound?"

She eyed me.

"It might be agreeable. Does it involve a burger?"

I grinned as I slid in bed next to her, pulling her against me and breathing in her scent. It had been a year since that day she had taken me back into her life and agreed to marry me. We hadn't gotten married yet, but the ring on her finger let everyone know that I fully planned on doing the deed just as soon as this mess was done.

Now we were living in the little house she had been renting, my shit all over the place. Together we had purchased the place and now were in the process of remodeling it together, something I found I enjoyed doing. Anything I did with her was enjoyable, and I found myself wondering from time to time what my life had been like during those years we weren't together. Sydney was my world, the very air I breathed, and every time she walked out of that door to go to work, I found myself panicking that she might not come back.

True to form, the chief had taken her back with open arms, putting her on the task force that was currently hunting down Grayson and his traitors. I joined in from the Horsemen side, but during work we kept it strictly professional between us. She had a job to do, and so did I.

That's why I was waiting to marry her. I wanted us to not have this black cloud hanging over us. Nuzzling her ear, I let my hands roam down her body.

"You know, I could make your afternoon pretty spectacular."

She laughed.

"You always do. What did you have in mind Zack?"

"A little bit of this," I said, squeezing her breast. "A little bit of that."

"I think that might be nice," she said breathlessly, arching against me.

I nibbled on her neck as my hand drifted lower, nearly finding the waistband of her shorts, before her cell phone buzzed on the bedside table, scaring us both.

"I got to get it," she sighed, stilling my hand.

"No, you don't, you're off for the weekend," I growled, resuming my trek. "Let it ring."

She stopped me again.

"But what if they have found Grayson?"

I sighed. Now that would be something we both would be interested in.

"Fine, but if they haven't, I get you for the entire weekend."

She patted my hand and reached over, looking at the message.

"Nope, no word."

I took the phone out of her hand and chunked it into the nearby pile of clothes on the floor.

"Good, you owe me a weekend."

Sydney grinned as I moved over her, touching my face with her hand.

"Well then, do your worst."

EPILOGUE
Neil "Deadeye" Wheeler

Three hours from Cibolo

I drummed my fingers on the scarred table, watching each person as they walked into the bar. It was late afternoon, but the interior of the bar made it feel like night, the smoky atmosphere already full despite the time of day.

I hated bars. Even in my youth I had tended to stay away from them, not liking the claustrophobic feeling of having people crammed into a small space. As much as I would rather have been anywhere else than here, I was here for a reason.

A damn good one.

The waitress stopped by, a wide smile on her overly painted face.

"Another beer?"

"Sure," I said, handing her the empty bottle. "Bring two while you are at it darling."

She nodded, giving me a wink before disappearing in the crowd. She had already slipped me her number with the last beer, and as much as I could use a quick fuck outside, I had bigger things to do.

That, and I couldn't afford the distraction. After a year of hunting down my own brothers, traitors to the Horsemen name, I was starting to make headway on the road that led to Grayson Barnes.

Disgust crawled over my skin as I thought about the former vice president of the Devil's Horsemen. At one time I had looked up to him, as many of the younger members had. Hell, even Grant Travis had treated him like family, entrusting that his right-hand man had his back regardless of what happened.

But that hadn't been the case. Grayson, in an attempt to take over the top seat, had kidnapped Hayley Travis, Grant's youngest daughter, and gotten many of our brothers killed in the process. Some were still recovering, making our numbers pitifully slim.

I had been given the task of hunting down any traitors to the Horsemen name, and over the last year I had killed more than I cared to count. Guys I had once shared a beer with, some that had been good friends, staring at the end of the gun as I ended their life. Some had begged, but most had been resigned to the fact that the undocumented assassin for the DHMC had found them. Their traitorous ways could not go unpunished.

Shifting in the seat, I watched the crowd, looking for one in particular. He was supposedly Grayson's right-hand man now and would likely know where the former head was hiding. If I could find him, then I might end this year of bloodshed and heartache that night.

God knows I wanted to be done with it. Months on the road had taken its toll on me, and I was ready to be back home, moving on with my life.

The sound of a familiar laugh caught my ear and I turned, my blood turning to ice as I took in the familiar form. Shit. What was she doing here? Of all the things I could have seen, I hadn't anticipated seeing her.

Swallowing, I watched as she talked to the woman next to her, her long hair swaying to the music that played from the speakers overhead. I knew every inch of that body, every freckle that graced her skin. Even now my cock hardened against my jeans, remembering our times together as well.

I couldn't let her see me. Roxanne had been everything to me but also my own worst enemy, and we were apart for a damn good reason.

It wouldn't be good to drum up anything from that time, not today.

I stood and threw some bills on the table, pushing through the crowd as I headed for the exit. I would find the asshole another day.

"Deadeye Wheeler, what brings your ugly face around here?"

I turned and stared down the ugly biker in front of me.

"Who the hell are you?"

The biker sneered, showing his tobacco stained teeth.

"You don't remember me. That's fine. I am going to cut that tongue out of your lying mouth and feed it to my dogs."

I held up my hands as he pulled out a knife, a sneer crossing my face.

"I'm sure you don't want to do that, partner."

"Oh, I want to do that and more," he said, passing the knife from hand to hand. "You killed my brother, and I have been waiting a long time to get revenge."

Great. This is not what I needed.

The patrons of the bar were backing away as I pulled my own knife, seeing no recourse other than to kill the fucker and move on. The glint in his eye told me that he would bury the knife in my back the moment I turned away from him, which only gave me one option.

"You want some?" I asked with a feral grin. "Come get some."

The biker growled and lunged with his knife. I sidestepped him and watched as he stumbled to catch his balance, palming my knife lightly in my own hand. By the looks of it, I was going to be shedding his fucker's blood all over this bar in a matter of minutes.

He snarled and lunged at me again, but again not fast enough.

"Give it up," I challenged him as he stumbled into the crowd. "Don't make me kill you."

"You don't have a soul!" he shouted. "You killed my brother in cold blood."

"Your brother was an asshole," I growled, not even sure who his brother was at this point.

I didn't make it a point to know all their names or their faces, only that I had gotten the job done and moved on. That was what Grant Travis was paying me to do.

"Looks like it runs in the family."

He lunged, and I caught him midair, slamming my knife into his belly and feeling the immediate warmth of his blood on my hands. The man made a sound, but I ignored it, pulling out the knife and letting him fall to the floor. A gut wound was a nasty one, but I doubted it would kill him.

If he got treatment in time.

"Y-you stabbed me!" he wailed as I wiped my knife on my jeans and sheathed it back into place.

"That's what happens when you play with knives," I muttered, looking at the horrified faces staring back at me. "Enjoy your afternoon folks."

Stalking toward the door, I could feel everyone's eyes on my back, the tension in the room thick enough to… well, cut with a knife. There would be stories, but no one would call the cops on this one. Hell, half the room was wanted by the cops anyway.

A motion caught my eye and I found myself staring at Roxanne, my bloodied hand on the door. Her eyes were cold, not full of the warmth I had been used to all those years ago, with no hint of tenderness on her gorgeous face. I didn't bother to smile a her, knowing what was running through her mind about me.

"Rox."

She gave a hollow laugh.

"Seems you haven't changed one-bit, Neil."

I shook my head.

"Were you expecting someone different?"

She crossed her arms over her chest, her generous breasts shifting with the movement and threatening to spill out of her top. Damn she looked great and smelled even better.

"No," she bit out. "Once a killer, always a killer."

I gave her a slight grin as I pushed open the door, letting the sunlight into the dim interior.

"What you see is what you get sweetheart. You look good, Rox."

She made a strangled sound as I walked out into the hot Texas heat. I would see her again, no doubt about it.

END OF BOOK 1

Because reviews help spread word about my books, please leave a brief review on Amazon or Goodreads if you enjoyed *WRECKED*. Thank you!

FREE BOOK: Sign up for my newsletter and download my bestselling standalone MC romance LOGAN. Available FREE only at http://brookwilder.com/logan/

BOOK 2: Read on for preview of the next full-length steamy standalone story of the *Devil's Horsemen MC* trilogy: SHATTERED!

PREVIEW: SHATTERED

Rox

I stood at the back door, feeling a world of emotions swirling around in my body, threatening to overcome me at any moment. I had put this off for four months, dealing with my grief in ways I didn't want to even think about. When people said there was a step-by-step process to grief, I had never believed them, thinking it was some crock of shit to get the whole therapy business going.

But now… well, I probably needed some therapy at this moment.

I straightened my shoulders, fiddling around with inserting the key into the lock. I didn't have to do this by myself. More than one person had offered to come with me, to even do it themselves, but I knew my brother would not want strangers rifling through his stuff.

As if he would care now.

Turning the key, I pushed open the door, and the immediate smell of stale cigarettes hit me full force. Leo had never been one to smoke outside, much preferring to do it wherever he was standing.

"Why the fuck would I want to smoke while freezing my balls off?" he had asked me once. "It's my damn house. I can smoke in there if I want to."

I hadn't disagreed. It was his house, after all. It was understood that you would come out smelling like an ash tray after a visit. I had given him hell about it of course, being his younger bratty sister. I got more middle fingers than I cared to mention, always done with love.

But I wouldn't have that happen now. I wouldn't see his grin when I came over to have our weekly supper, nor would I hear him call me 'Red', a nod to my fiery red hair.

Tears clouded my vision as I stepped inside and shut the door, taking a moment to allow the tears to flow down my cheeks. Leo

Tate had been everything to me, my only sibling, whom I'd looked up to dearly. He had been my best friend, my rock, and though we both hadn't had an easy childhood, it had been Leo that had protected me from our father's fists, Leo who had taken the blows himself, so I could escape.

Who was going to protect me now?

Sliding down the door, I sat on the cold tile of the kitchen, staring at the doorway that led to the rest of his small house. Any minute, he was going to come around that corner and laugh at me for crying like this. Any minute, he was going to scoop me up in one of his famous hugs.

Why had he died instead of me? The pain… I couldn't take it. There had been a moment after his death when my life had fallen apart, when I had considered joining him. I had no family other than him, nothing in my life that meant a damn. It would have been too easy to take some pills or drown myself in my bathtub and just give up.

But there had been a small voice that nagged me every time I had considered it, urging me to fight in his name and never let this earth forget Leo Tate.

Wiping my face with my hand, I picked myself up off the floor and walked over to the cabinet to locate a trash bag, so that I could start my clean out. Four months this house had sat silent, and over the last few weeks I had started to think about moving in. My crap apartment was the size of a closet, and I knew that Leo's house was paid off, paid with cash that I knew had come from his time with the motorcycle club, The Devil's Horsemen. The club had been everything to my brother, the family we'd never had, and there had been a moment… well, I thought I could have been a part of that family as well.

Anger filled my veins as I yanked open the fridge and started dumping the spoiled food into the trash bag. There had been a time in my life when I'd thought everything was lining up for the Tate children. Leo was happy, and I had finally gotten with the man I thought would make me just as happy.

But that had not been the case. In fact, Neil Wheeler was the reason Leo was not here in this house today.

Blowing out a breath, I moved on to the drawers in the fridge, throwing away anything that was in there as well. Seeing Neil two weeks ago had been a jolt to my entire body, sending me hurtling back to the days that were not full of pain and anguish. My heart had stopped as I took in his muscular form, dressed in his customary black outfit. I had sworn to him at one time that he had no color in his closet, even going as far as to buy him a shirt that reminded me of his eyes.

Oh, those eyes… They were a show-stopper.

"No," I said aloud to an empty house.

I wasn't going there. After years of lusting after Neil, I had succeeded in getting his attention and ultimately into my bed.

And it had cost me everything.

Finishing the fridge, I put the bag by the door and forced myself to walk down the hall, pausing at Leo's bedroom. I was going to give nearly all of his clothes to the thrift shop, keeping only a few pieces for myself. In fact, there would only be a few things of my brother's I would keep. I wanted to turn this house into a place for me and not a shrine to him. At some point, I had to move on from his death.

The bed was still unmade, the covers thrown on the floor as if my brother had just crawled out of it. I sighed as I walked over and laid my hand on the covers, the cold seeping through my skin. That day I'd got the call, I had been at my beauty shop not far from here.

It had been the worst day of my life.

"Oh, Leo!" I whispered. "What were you doing?"

Silence greeted me. My brother had been dumped in a ditch outside town, still wearing his DHMC vest. I had that vest, bloodstain and all, back in my apartment, tucked away in a box. The club had been such a huge part of his life, and I knew he wouldn't want me to burn it, though I wanted to. I wanted to burn the entire club down, along with a few people inside. They had turned their back on my brother, and one of their own had killed them.

The one I had least expected to do something like that.

Sitting down on the bed, I placed my head in my hands, the memories of my childhood hitting me flat in the face. Neil Wheeler had lived next door to us. Leo and Neil had been good friends growing up, getting into trouble together and planning one day to be part of one of the bike gangs in Cibolo, Texas.

I, on the other hand, was the gangly little sister, with stars in her eyes every time I interacted with Neil Wheeler. My crush on him literally started from birth, and even though he didn't give me any indication that he would be interested in me one day, I hadn't given up.

Especially the time my brother found out about my little crush.

***

'Roxanne Wheeler'.

'Roxy Wheeler'.

'Rox Wheeler'.

I frowned as I looked at the doodles on the page. While 'Roxanne' sounded so sophisticated, 'Roxy' was sexy.

And if I was to be with Neil, I had to be sexy.

The problem was, I had no curves like the girls I had seen him with lately. He clearly preferred big boobs and a butt to match, and I had neither.

I doubted he was going to go for my charming personality, or the fact that I could tell him all his favorite things, from his food to the shows he liked to watch on TV. I knew everything about Neil Wheeler, everything.

My bedroom door burst open, and I froze on the bed, half expecting my father to storm into the room. He was still pissed about the grades I had brought him yesterday, and while Leo had stopped him from hitting me, I knew it was only going to be a matter of time before he got his hands on me.

"You scared me," I scolded my brother, sitting up.

"Sorry," Leo said, grinning. "I just wanted to tell you that I won't be home tonight."

A shiver of fear ran through me, knowing what that meant for me. I would have to bolt my door tonight.

"What are you doing?"

He shook his head as he walked to the bed, sitting next to me.

Leo was seventeen, and I knew I would be lucky to have him another year in this home. Once he left, there would only be me and my mom to take the brunt of my father's wrath.

"You don't need to know that. It's probably better you don't, so if someone asks, you won't have to lie."

I gave him a little shrug. Then it must be something dangerous or illegal. He shifted, and my notebook fell on the floor.

"I'll get it," I said quickly.

He got there first, picking it up and reading the contents on the page.

"What the hell is this, Red?"

My cheeks burned.

"It's nothing, just some doodling. Give it back."

He held it just out of my reach, his gaze narrowed.

"You have a thing for Neil."

"I-I do not," I said with very little conviction, as I reached for the notebook.

"Yes, you do," he breathed. "How have I not seen this before now?"

I crossed my arms over my chest, giving him a look.

"It's nothing, alright?"

"It better be," he said, throwing the notebook on the bed. "You don't belong with any of us, Rox. You are too good for this town, for the likes of Neil Wheeler."

I stared at him.

"B-but he's your best friend."

Leo gave a shrug, walking to the door.

"But he's not good enough for my baby sister. Keep this door barred tonight, Rox. I'll be back in the morning. Love ya!"

"Love ya!" I echoed as he walked out of the room, shutting the door behind him.

Leo was wrong. Neil was the perfect guy for me.

***

I shook out of my thoughts. Maybe my brother had been right all along about Neil. He had done nothing but broken my heart and ripped my brother from me. Neil was a sniper for the DHMC, and when Neil's body had been examined, it hadn't been difficult at all to know who had fired the fatal bullet.

I hated him.

Rising from the bed, I started toward Leo's dresser, tripping over a box in the middle of the floor in the process. The contents spilled out onto the carpet and I knelt down, shuffling through the papers. An envelope slid out from my grasp, and my blood ran cold as I saw my name scrawled on the front in my brother's handwriting.

I dropped the other papers on the floor and snatched up the envelope, my hands shaking as I looked at it. Leo had never been one to be sentimental; he'd gotten me a gun for my eighteenth birthday, instead of a birthday card.

This would have to have been something very important for him to have taken the time to prepare it. There was only one way to find out.

I sat back on the bed and slit the envelope, extracting the single piece of paper out of its holding place. My eyes blurred as I opened it, recognizing my brother's handwriting. With a deep breath, I started to read.

Enjoyed the preview? SHATTERED will be available soon!

OTHER BOOKS BY BROOK WILDER

GHOST RIDERS MC SERIES
BOUGHT
SHACKLED

DEVIL'S MARTYRS MC SERIES
DEVIL'S DEAL
DEVIL'S SEED
DEVIL'S BARGAIN
DEVIL'S PACT
DEVIL'S VOW
DEVIL'S PASSION

CONTARINI CRIME FAMILY SERIES
CLAIMED BY THE DON
CHAINED BY THE DON
BOUND BY THE DON

BROKEN HOUNDS MC SERIES
RENEGADE
REVENGE
REDEMPTION

Made in the USA
Monee, IL
21 January 2020